Readers love CAITLIN RICCI

To the Highest Bidder

"This was a wonderfully written book."

—MM Good Book Reviews

"…it was a solid story with an interesting plot hook. I will admit, I found the brief epilogue emotionally rewarding, too."

—Joyfully Jay

"...I can assuredly say I will be checking out more of her work in the future."

—The Novel Approach

Country Strong

"Caitlin Ricci knows how to craft characters that seem to leap from the pages of the book. There is an honesty to the storytelling that makes the writing seem less like a fiction…"

—Sensual Reads

Marked by Grief

"…a touching, heartbreaking, and loving story that I truly enjoyed."
—Prism Book Alliance

"*Marked by Grief* is the sort of book you want to read in one sitting…"
—Love Romances & More

By CAITLIN RICCI

Country Strong
Cuddling (Dreamspinner Anthology)
His Lion Tamer
Marked by Grief
One More Time
To the Highest Bidder

A FOREVER HOME
Rescuing Jack
Of Monsters and Men

Published by Harmony Ink Press
First Time for Everything (Harmony Ink Anthology)
Weathering the Storm

Published by DREAMSPINNER PRESS
www.dreamspinnerpress.com

One *More* Time

Caitlin Ricci

DREAMSPINNER
PRESS

Published by
DREAMSPINNER PRESS

5032 Capital Circle SW, Suite 2, PMB# 279, Tallahassee, FL 32305-7886 USA
www.dreamspinnerpress.com

One More Time
© 2015 Caitlin Ricci.

Cover Art
© 2015 Caitlin Ricci.
Cover content is for illustrative purposes only and any person depicted on the cover is a model.

ISBN: 978-1-63476-298-4
Digital ISBN: 978-1-63476-299-1
Library of Congress Control Number: 2015943928
First Edition September 2015

Printed in the United States of America
∞
This paper meets the requirements of
ANSI/NISO Z39.48-1992 (Permanence of Paper).

This one goes out to my best friend and biggest supporter, my husband, Scott. I love you, babe.

Welcome to Thornwood, Colorado. Please enjoy your stay.

CHAPTER ONE

Caleb

I LOOKED up from unpacking the box at my feet at the sound of the doorbell ringing. It was a soft chime, which I was glad about because I hadn't thought to check it before deciding to buy the house. When the bell sounded again, I straightened up and instantly grabbed at my lower back. There was some rule about not bending over boxes and lifting with my legs instead of my bad back, but I'd apparently forgotten my doctor's orders in the move. I'd be paying for that by sundown, I was sure. I hurried to answer it, checked the peephole, and decided to open the heavy wooden door anyway, despite my better judgement. The kitchen was close, and I was pretty sure I'd managed to unpack the knives already if the cop on the other side of the door ended up being some kind of backwoods small-town Colorado murderer or something.

"Can I help you, officer?" I asked. I tried not to pay attention to how cute he was, which was damn hard given his smile. I was always a sucker for a good smile. And a cup of coffee just like the one he extended toward me.

"Hey. I'm Trent, and please don't call me 'officer' unless I'm arresting you. Everyone calls me by my first name."

I accepted the coffee and held it up so I could sniff it. I am fairly certain I sighed because he grinned at me like he was trying not to laugh. "Sorry." I was blushing pretty badly, judging by how warm the tops of my ears felt. "I haven't unpacked my coffee machine yet. Thanks for this. Is there something wrong?" I asked, because in Los

1

Angeles cops didn't randomly come to my door unless there was trouble. I'd only been in Thornwood a day, and now I had a cop at my door. My sister, Marie, would probably love to know what kind of trouble I'd managed to get myself into so soon.

Trent shook his head, his hat slipping a little, and I was momentarily distracted by his dark hair. It was the color of chocolate, which, like my coffee, I hadn't unpacked either. I'd barely managed to get a towel out for my shower that morning after making sure my books were out on the bookshelf. "Nothing's wrong. Why? Do you think there is?"

I shrugged and sipped the coffee. Cream and sugar, which I could handle, though I normally took it black. At least he hadn't grabbed me a latte or something else that would put me in a sugar coma before lunch. "There's a cop on my front porch," I pointed out, as if my concerns needed to be explained.

"Oh!" Understanding seemed to come to him instantly. "Oh, no. I'm not here because you did something. Unless you did?"

"Not that I know of," I replied, wondering what he was doing there if it wasn't because of something I'd done.

Trent smiled at me. "Then you're fine. I just wanted to come here and introduce myself. Meet the new neighbor kind of thing."

"Really?"

"Yeah. It's a small town. So...." He shifted his weight as he leaned back on his heels. "You waiting on your family to move here too?"

I shook my head and knew why he was asking that. I'd bought a massive house, because I'd wanted to and had been able to afford it after the settlement from a car accident. But I'd probably be getting the family question fairly often until people got over their curiosity about the new guy in town. "Nope. Just me."

"Horses?"

"None of those either."

He frowned at me and turned to look over the barn and pastures that had come with the property. "You know you bought a horse farm, right?"

2

I laughed and took another sip of the coffee. It really was nice of him to bring it for me. "Yeah. I know. You want to come in or something?"

It was the first time I'd ever actually invited a cop into my home, not that I'd ever had anything to hide, but in LA I used to get told about probable cause and warrants all the time from my neighbors. It had been normal conversation over getting the mail. I hadn't been living in the best neighborhood at the time.

Trent chewed on his bottom lip, and damn I wanted to kiss him, but that would have been insanity. He shook his head as he stopped messing with his lip, and I got a break from thinking about kissing him for a bit. "Thanks, but I should probably be getting to work. Here's my number, in case you need something." He dug a business card out of his pocket and put his coffee down on my porch to write his number on it.

I took the card, though I wasn't too sure why I did so. It wasn't like I'd be calling him or anything. "Don't you have 911 up here?" Thornwood couldn't possibly have been so tiny that the emergency services required me calling Trent up.

"Yeah, we've got 911. Where'd you think you moved to? Antarctica or something?"

He smiled again, and I barely managed to shrug while I stood there staring at him like a dumbass. Damn but he was cute in that navy-blue uniform. I wanted to see him out of it.

"Just call. And what's your name? I don't think I caught it."

I shook my head. "I didn't say it. Caleb Robinson."

"See you later, Caleb," he told me as I stepped back, ready to close the door.

"Later."

He lifted his coffee to salute me, I did the same, and then he turned on his heel and went down the curving path through my front yard to where his police car was parked next to my very old and quite rusty SUV. Which, I realized a minute after he began pulling away, had expired tags. Damn. I tensed up, waiting for him to notice, but he didn't stop. Instead he just waved to me, I waved back at him, and then he was gone, and I went back to my morning of unpacking boxes and trying to move stuff around.

I'd never had a house this big, with five bedrooms and three bathrooms. A dozen acres spread around me, and I had no plans for any of it. Mostly I'd just wanted to get away from LA, from my life there, from everything that reminded me of that place.

I hadn't always hated it, though. I was a graphic designer, and I liked the busy lifestyle and the colors there. But dating my married boss had sort of put a damper on my love affair with the city.

My phone rang, and I hurried over to it, expecting to hear from my sister sometime that day, and instead seeing a familiar name staring back at me. "Hi." I swallowed thickly. "I didn't think I'd hear from you again."

"Hey. How's life in the mountains?" Paul asked. I'd had two months away from him, two months since I'd last been in his bed, since I'd last told him I loved him. I could still feel the scrape of his teeth on my collarbone and his fingertips digging into my hips as he fucked me.

"Thornwood isn't really in the mountains. More like the foothills," I said. I tried to keep things casual, to keep my voice light. But when I looked down at my hand on the island, I saw I was gripping it so hard my knuckles were white. I stepped back and shook out my hand. "I thought we'd agreed not to talk again."

"I know we did. But that was then and this is now. You've had some time to cool off. Give me another chance. I want to talk to you again. Why won't you let me?"

I sighed and flopped down on the couch, a foldout sofa bed monster I'd had since college, and looked out at the pine trees just beyond the huge windows that had made me fall in love with the house as soon as I walked in.

"Because...." I struggled to come up with a reasonable explanation that I hadn't already told him, but since there wasn't one, I went with the first. It hadn't worked last year when I tried to break it off with him though, so I wasn't sure why I brought it up again. "Because you were never going to leave your wife for me."

I heard Paul slam something, and this time I didn't jump, like I'd done all the time back in LA. "Caleb, you knew that. From the start of this, you knew I wasn't going to leave her. Her father owns the design firm. He pays my salary. He paid yours. My life would have been over if I'd left her."

I knew all of this, having heard it many times in the past. We'd been together for a while, nearly three years, and I thought I loved him. He'd said it often enough to me as well.

"Look, I'll be coming through Denver next month to meet with some new clients. Can I see you?"

There was so much hope in his voice, and I was tempted to give in, to tell him that he could come over, that I'd be waiting right here for him like I always was. But this was a new start for me. I'd chosen to move, to get on with my life, and I'd done it in a big way. I hadn't simply quit my job, or moved to a place he hadn't been in; I moved to another state. Another time zone even.

"I don't think so. Not this time," I said. And I was proud of myself for saying no, just this once. That had taken a lot for me to be able to do.

"Why not?"

I closed my eyes, then pinched the bridge of my nose. But my glasses got in the way and I ended up stabbing the little plastic pads into the corners of my eyes instead. Glasses were a new experience for me since more often than not I wore my contacts, but I hadn't felt like putting them in this morning when my eyes were so dry from the Colorado air. I desperately needed to pick up a humidifier to fix that.

"Because it's not a good idea. Because I'm not going to be the other man again. Not anymore. The sex was good, but I can't do it anymore. I want a real relationship and not one that involves being called into lunch meetings so you can get your dick sucked as I hide under the desk in case anyone happens to walk by."

He laughed as if he thought I was joking. Too bad I wasn't. At first it had been a little sexy, maybe, to have this kind of secret thing going on. I wasn't some innocent, naive person, though. I'd known who he was, and who his wife was, the first time we kissed while working late on a project. But somehow I'd been dumb enough to believe that he'd eventually realize I was better for him than she was. I hadn't taken into account how much more he loved his money than he cared about either her or me apparently.

"I'm being serious," I told him when he was still laughing at my nonexistent joke.

That shut him up quickly. "Oh. Well, why don't I come visit you, and we can see how we work out like that? You could be my Colorado love affair."

Saying no to that was easy, but the way he offered it made me wonder something. I should have asked it a long time ago, but I hadn't, and I wasn't sure why. Maybe I'd been too scared, too worried about the answer to find out for sure. But that wasn't the case any longer. "How many other men were you having sex with while we were together?" I asked in a clipped tone, because I was sure I wasn't the only one. Not with how he so easily suggested that I be his Colorado affair, like he had a guy waiting for him in every state. He likely did actually.

"Caleb…. C'mon, you know it's not like that. You were special to me. You still are."

"How many others?" I asked. "More than ten? More than twenty?"

He took a long time answering me. "Thirty-six, I guess. I haven't really kept track."

"Jesus fucking Christ!" I suddenly felt really ill, and I was glad I'd been getting tested regularly for all of my adult life.

"Caleb, that's just a number. You know they didn't mean anything to me. They—"

I shook my head. "Paul, stop. It's over. It was over between us when I quit my job, it was over when your wife hit me with her car

6

after finding out about us, it was over when I left California, and it sure as hell is over now! Don't try to call me again. I won't pick up. Just... damn. Go get some help or something. Bye."

I hung up my phone before he could say anything else to me, and I was glad I had, because soon enough I was bent over my toilet heaving up the coffee Trent had brought me, which was the only thing I'd bothered to have so far that morning. Lucky for me.

After my throw-up session, I desperately needed a hot shower too. I couldn't believe it. Well, actually I probably could. Paul was smooth and slick like a model in a magazine. I'd been falling all over myself around him since the first time he touched my hand when I went in for an interview.

Saying yes to him the first time wasn't hard to do. And it got easier as we went along. Sex in his office, in his car, in a hotel, in my apartment... they were all normal parts of my life with him. He would send me a text saying he needed a file brought over, and a location, and I would be there.

I'd missed parties with friends, phone calls from my sister, and important meetings with my own clients just to be his fuck toy basically. It hurt to realize that now, but for once I was finally thinking with a clear head, and things were actually looking up for me, now that I didn't have Paul Diggs around to screw with my thoughts and my body.

It was a good feeling to be free of him, and when I'd gotten cleaned up, I was ready to go explore Thornwood. I'd brought food with me, of a sort, in the form of beef jerky, bottles of soda, and granola bars. But now I was hungry for something real. I felt a little bad for leaving a pile of boxes half-unpacked in the middle of what would be a gorgeous living room once my clutter and broken pieces of cardboard were removed. But then again, this was my house now, my first house, the first time I hadn't been living in an apartment, and if I wanted to leave cardboard boxes lying around, then I could. I was able to leave them there for weeks if I chose to. Uh, actually, no I couldn't. That would drive me nuts. But I could wait to unpack the rest of them for a little while. I'd been pushing hard to get through them all in one day. I could take a little break. And my back was really sore too. I rubbed at it as I walked down the narrow, winding path that went from my front door to the driveway. Another path went to an old garage, but I didn't think I'd be using it all that often until it got really cold and snowy. My SUV was good off-road—it had perpetual mud on it—and I couldn't remember a time when I'd ever kept it in a garage except for at work. And I hadn't made enough to make that an affordable everyday option.

My SUV and I bumped along the uneven dirt driveway that ran into my property until it met up with a paved two-lane road, which I understood to be the main street going through Thornwood. Tiny towns were new to me, but I absolutely loved the lack of traffic as I signaled out of habit, then pulled onto the road. I turned on some classic rock—my favorite—and kept to the speed limit as much as I could since the way was a bit twisty and I didn't really know my way all that well.

I passed by what looked like a pretty nice horse property a few miles down the road with a sign saying they gave lessons and offered boarding. There was even a sign for an upcoming competition, which made me think of my nephews, who were all big into showing their horses. It wasn't something I'd ever been interested in, and my sister hadn't been either, but I guessed her husband was in a big way. I wasn't all that close to him, probably because the only thing we had in common was my sister and the kids, but I'd been trying. Now that I had a house, I planned to invite them out to spend some time there. I was pretty sure I'd get tired of having three boys running around my home pretty quickly. I wasn't really big on kids for the most part, but since I hadn't seen them since before the oldest one started kindergarten, and now he was a teenager, I thought I probably should. They were my nephews after all, and I missed my sister.

I drove into what I figured was the town proper, which was little more than ten stores all together on either side of the street, parking spots in front of them, and signs for more parking behind the stores in the aspens. I saw a mechanic, a bank, a drug store, a craft place, a pet store, which promised the lowest prices of tropical fish around, a fishing store with live bait, and then, at the end of the row and with the most cars circled around it, a fifties era-looking diner complete with aluminum accents and neon lights.

I parked in front of the diner, which was called Rosie's, and headed inside. Seating was tight, but I got a space at a high bar with people sitting on stools on either side of me. Like a typical diner, the place was loud, but the food looked great—or maybe that was because I was starving. Either way I needed a bacon cheeseburger right away.

After my food came and some of my need dissipated as I took big bites of my burger and shoved fries into my mouth, I looked around the diner and noticed a familiar face. The only person I knew in town was talking with some other cops in a booth. When he saw me looking, I waved to him, he waved back, and I returned to my burger. The food was great, with just the right amount of grease coming out of my thick burger patty and dripping down my fingers as I ate. I knew I'd be back there regularly, and not just because it looked to be the only place in town to eat out. From where I was seated, with big windows a few seats down from me, I could see a small grocery store tucked behind some of the aspens farther on through town, which was great because that meant I could get frozen pizzas to keep on hand. I wouldn't be doing much cooking. I just wasn't all that good at it. Thankfully I already had design jobs line up from clients back in LA who were just waiting for me to open my books and become available again. I'd be booked solid again in a month, I was sure of it, and that was a good feeling.

I'd always loved to create beautiful things for other people, but doing so while also worrying about my relationship with Paul had been a bit of a mess. Now I could do my job and make banners and websites for people without having to worry about any complications like that.

"Hey, Caleb."

I looked up to see Trent standing next to me. "Hi." I wiped my mouth with my napkin and wanted to invite him to sit down, but the seats around me were full of people eating lunch just like I was. "On break?" I asked instead.

He nodded. "Yeah. Glad you made it out of your house to come mingle with the townsfolk."

I smiled and he smiled back at me. "It's good food."

"Better be. Rosie was my mom."

I thought he was joking at first, but he just kept looking at me, and I slowly realized he wasn't joking at all. "Wow. Uh, congrats."

"Thanks."

"Trent, we gotta go! Break's over, kid!" one of the guys with him called.

Trent turned and waved to them but not before I could see him blushing, maybe at being called a kid. He couldn't have been that far from my own age of thirty-two, but maybe since the guys with him looked to be in their fifties, that was why they referred to him with that particular appellation.

"See you around," I told him.

He nodded. "Yeah. You will."

There was nothing ominous in the way he'd said it, just a simple, yes, I would. Probably because he was a cop and they were pretty active in the small town. He touched my shoulder as he left, nothing too major but enough for me to know he'd done it. I brushed it off, figuring it was a small town and people were probably pretty friendly.

But after I was done with lunch and spent some time walking around the town, I was thinking about it and wondering why he'd touched me like that. It was hard for me not to wonder, but as I drove back to my new house to tackle the boxes in my living room a few hours later, it started to get easier to forget about the touch and move on.

I found a picture of my sister and her kids and put it up on my bookcase in the living room, right next to my copy of the biography of Harvey Milk. I had romances galore, a lot of them historicals, under that shelf, but that was where I kept my important stuff. I put a geode next to the book, a small one, barely more than two inches wide, that I'd held on to since the first boy I ever kissed had given it to me. Right before his dad had broken us apart, then moved him to the other side of the country. I'd been thirteen.

A little jade elephant—a gift from my sister that she'd found in a shop in Thailand well before she met Dan and had the kids— was placed next to her picture. She'd traveled the world while I was getting my degree in design. I'd been jealous of her, but she was just as jealous of me when she went back to school after her travels, only to find out that she was the oldest person in her freshman class. And though some of the teachers liked her, none of the guys in her classes did.

With my bookshelf done, I had one more box I could recycle in the morning. It was a long drive to the nearest dump that had a recycling center, close to half an hour, but I didn't want to throw them away, and I couldn't stand all the clutter. I'd had movers to help me with the big stuff, but I'd gone from an apartment to a huge house and most of my big stuff fit in one room. I'd been sleeping on the fold-out couch in the living room since my futon stopped flipping back up to a couch a few months back, and as I sat down on it and groaned, I realized I really didn't want to do any more moving, ever. I hated it. Not only was I not fit enough to carry heavy boxes everywhere, but my back hurt from bending over for even a short amount of time. If I wasn't careful with it, my doctor in LA had told me, I'd throw it out for sure. I needed to find a good chiropractor, and soon, before I wound up on the floor on my stomach, unable to move again like I had in LA.

I was mostly done unpacking my kitchen when I heard something get knocked over by the garage, which I brushed off without thinking much about it. I really only heard it because I didn't have on any music. Otherwise the house was completely silent except for me moving things around. I needed to get my TV hooked up right away to fix that. I couldn't stand the quiet after living for so long in the city.

But I heard the noise again, and after freezing and wondering where it came from, I walked over to the big windows across from my sofa bed to check if I could see anything outside. I couldn't exactly see the garage, and even if I could, it was dark out and I didn't have any outside lights.

I had been used to sleeping by the light of an overhead streetlamp across from me that lit up the parking lot where impounded vehicles were taken. I shook my head as I realized, for the first time really, that moving here had not been my smartest idea ever. I didn't even own a flashlight.

I heard something coming from the garage again and dug my phone out of my pocket to call 911. I probably should have too, but I pulled out Trent's card with his number on it, and suddenly I was dialing him while I crouched beside my window and hoped that whoever it was out there hadn't seen me standing in my living room all alone with the lights on behind me.

"Hello, this is Trent," he answered on the third ring.

"Trent!" I hissed into the phone as I covered it and my mouth with my hand to muffle the sound of my voice. "It's Caleb—"

"I know who you are. There aren't that many people in this town that I can't remember the voices of. What's wrong?"

I heard him getting up, and the sound of a bed squeaking, and I winced, hoping I hadn't woken him up or interrupted something. It was only nine, but maybe he had to be up early. I wanted to hang up, to tell him I'd only been imagining something being by my garage, but then I thought back to every single horror movie that took place in a cabin in the woods where not one of those stupid kids ever called a cop at the first sign of something going wrong. Well, I had a cop on the phone with me right then, and I wasn't going to end up hacked into a bunch of little pieces if I could help it. "There's someone outside my house—"

"I'll be right there. Where are you? Are you safe?"

I couldn't tell if having him sounding genuinely worried about me was a good thing or not. "I'm in my living room, kneeling on the floor and trying not to be seen."

"Good. I'm getting in my car now. I'll check it out, then come up to the house. Stay on the phone with me."

"Okay, okay. I can do that." Breathing became easier as I relaxed a little bit. Trent was coming, he had a gun, and he would take care of whatever it was. "But what if it's a bear?" He couldn't possibly hold off a bear with just a gun.

He laughed, and I heard the sound of his car as he started driving. "If it's a bear, we've both got big problems."

"Well that's not reassuring at all," I grumbled.

"Wasn't supposed to be. I'm coming down the hill now. I'll be there in just a few minutes."

I nodded and licked my lips as I pressed my hand against the cold glass window. "Be careful."

"Will do."

CHAPTER TWO

Trent

I PULLED up to Caleb's house, which was more like a mansion compared to the rest of the houses in town. We didn't really have neighborhoods in Thornwood, just the town, and everyone lived in it. But Caleb's house was on the far east side of it and I lived directly in the center of the townhouses that stood between my mom's diner and the grocery store. I got a text and glanced down at it before I parked my car in Caleb's driveway.

Where'd you go? The bed's cold.

I shook my head and sent a quick text back. Neediness didn't really work for me, as endearing as my current bedmate thought it might be.

Out on a call.

There was no text of him telling me to be safe or to be careful or any of that, which didn't really surprise me. I'd found him on one of those quick hookup sites and was actually kind of surprised he decided to stay for a while after we were done. Most of the time the guys I brought home didn't.

Anyway, couldn't think about that right then. Caleb had someone by his house, and I was ready to rush in and save him, though I was pretty sure it was nothing. City boy might think we had bears, but I hadn't seen one around the town in at least a year. Deer on the other hand we had plenty of, elk too. But not bear.

I went around his house along the path toward the garage that could have easily fit my house inside it. Actually it probably was a barn at one time that someone had converted somewhere along the way. I hadn't been particularly close to the Smiths, who had owned the property before Caleb, but I did think it was a shame he didn't have horses in the fields like the Smiths had. I grew up seeing the foals playing each summer in those pastures.

The area around the garage was dark, which was something Caleb should have probably looked into, and I figured I'd mention it to him at some point. I had my gun out of the holster and held firmly between my hands, but just as I suspected, there was nothing for him to be worried about, just some knocked-over trash cans. No trash was in them, but there was probably the smell of old trash on them and I saw plenty of raccoon paw prints around.

With a shake of my head, I holstered my gun and went back up the trail to the house. I knocked on the door, waited a little while, then knocked again until I heard Caleb moving around in the house. He had all the lights off but with there being a full moon out and the house mostly made up of big glass windows like in one of those pretty magazines my mom had liked, it wasn't hard to track his movements inside the house. I even saw when he ran into a box and I heard him cursing as he opened up the front door.

"Hi, officer," he said as he pulled the door open. He looked around the house toward the garage, and I turned to look with him.

"You have raccoons, a few of them probably. Make sure your trash lids are tight, and you'll be fine, though they may make a mess of things sometimes." I shrugged.

Cleaning up after the raccoons were done was just par for the course as far as I figured. I was born in Denver, but we'd always lived in the mountains. They were home for me, and I was used to seeing more foxes than dogs around town, though we sure had plenty of both.

"Are they dangerous?" City Boy asked.

I smiled and shook my head. "Not really. Well, if one bites you, then maybe. It'll need to be tested, and if it's rabid, you'll need to get shots. But you should be fine."

15

He looked instantly more relieved. "Well, that's great. Yeah. Okay. So, you want to come in for a beer?"

I shouldn't have, because I had someone back home waiting on me to come back to bed. But.... Damn, what was his name? Sexyboy83 wasn't it, though that's what I'd known him as online. Beard Man wasn't it either, though he did have one. Whatever. I couldn't remember his name. And Caleb *was* offering me a beer. I nodded. "Sure. A beer would be good."

"Okay, then." Caleb stepped aside and I came in. He turned on the lights, and I blinked a few times, getting used to the light, while he fumbled around until he got to the fridge and pulled out some bottles. "I've been to the gas station but not the grocery store yet. I have jerky, beer, and that's about it. I think I'll be eating at the diner a lot."

I laughed and took the beer he handed me. "Yeah, most people do. I'm there most days on my lunch break. It's the unofficial cop spot, I guess."

"Good to know. Note to self: don't rob the diner," Caleb said, then nearly dropped his beer, as if he hadn't meant to say that aloud.

I laughed and shook my head at his shocked expression. "Yeah, not a good choice of places." I sat myself on one of the stools that were at the big island and watched him fumble with his words as I drank my beer. My phone went off, and I pulled it out of my pocket to check the text.

Hey dude, you dead or what?

Smiling, I sent a quick text back. *Yep.*

Fucker.

I wanted to laugh but instead put my phone back in my pocket. I sure did pick winners to bring home. At least they were just one-night kinds of guys and neither one of us had any sort of expectations. Those were tricky, useless things I didn't play with anymore.

"Everything okay?" Caleb asked. "You don't have to run off to another call or something?"

I shook my head. "Everything's good. Just someone saying hi." I got off the stool and began looking around the kitchen and

16

living room, since I was nosy but also because I wanted to know what kind of a guy bought a massive house far away from any major city, just to have it for himself.

Growing up, this place—Rocky Creek Stables, as it was once known before the Smiths retired from renting horses to tourists and just bred their horses instead—was somewhere that we kids always wanted to go. There was a horse place down the road, but they were always snobby to us when all we wanted to do was come pet the horses and feed them carrots and apples we saved from the snacks our parents sent us to school with. My mom had thought I suddenly started loving carrots when Mrs. Smith let us come feed the horses, and I asked for extras every day until she caught on.

Caleb followed me over to a bookshelf that had caught my attention. A picture of a pretty woman stood next to a little elephant statue. "Wife?" I asked.

"Sister," he corrected.

I nodded and kept looking, though I stopped at the biography of someone I'd heard of and also pulled out a romance novel just to confirm. Two guys lay together kissing on the cover. I put it away before turning back to him. "So, you're gay I take it."

He leaned against the wall and took a sip of his beer. "I am."

He looked kind of uncomfortable, maybe because he thought I was going to be judging him, but I just grinned. "Well, then, as the only out person I know of in this town, welcome to Thornwood. Your nearest gay bar worth going to is about an hour east of here in Denver, but the traffic typically isn't all that bad so sometimes you can make it in closer to forty minutes if you're lucky."

"You're out?" he asked. "And you're gay?" he added that last part on, though I thought he should have asked it first.

I nodded. I'd been out since I was a kid.

"And no one cares?" he continued, as if it were some foreign concept he couldn't quite grasp.

"If anyone cared there was a gay cop in town and actually made a fuss, my dad would have something pretty substantial to say about it," I said as I stepped away from the bookshelf to come join him against the wall.

"Why? He a mountain mob boss or something?" Caleb joked.

I laughed and shook my head. "No, but some people might think he is. He's the chief."

Caleb blushed, and I wondered if I could get him to go any darker or if the faint trail of pink over his cheeks that ran down his neck was as dark as he tended to get.

Either way, I wanted him. And not just a little bit. I full-on wanted him under me as he lay stretched out over my bed. His dark blond hair was a few inches long, and I wondered how it would look on my pillows and how much his face would flush as I went down on him.

I was getting hard just thinking about it, but then I felt a bit guilty since I'd had a guy in my bed before coming over. I couldn't really help being attracted to Caleb, but I could keep from being an asshole by not coming on to him the same night. Plus, I'd known him less than a day. Maybe he had someone waiting to come over to Colorado with him.

I'd find out sooner or later, because as a cop it was my business to know what was going on in my town. But I wasn't going to stand here with a hard dick pretending I didn't want Caleb to get down on his knees for me and make it all better. So I quickly downed the last of my beer, handed him my empty bottle, and then moved toward the front door.

"Thanks for the drink," I told him. "Take care, and be wary of strange raccoons."

Caleb chuckled and followed me to the door. "Thanks for coming by to check it out for me and making sure I was safe."

"Sure thing. Thanks for calling me. Good night."

He waved to me as I went down the trail to my car. I waved to him from beside his SUV and turned on my flashlight so I didn't trip on my way back to my car. His expired tags would need fixing, but I wouldn't mention it to him for another month. I still probably wouldn't give him a ticket, though. In such a small community, we didn't really like giving out tickets to our neighbors.

I drove back to my house, one of the little townhomes that stood in a row just off the main street. I could walk to the store, and if I didn't get a load of groceries, I could get myself just as easily to the diner too. I was pretty low on supplies though, so I'd need to take my car the next time I went. I was expecting to have my house to myself when I got there, but I found the bearded guy still naked, still waiting for me on my bed when I came in the front door. With my bedroom door open I could see him as soon as I crossed over the threshold of my little townhouse. Most of them were at least two bedrooms but I'd gone with the cheapest option.

"I thought you'd be gone before I got back," I said as I began taking off my holster and badge and locking them up.

He got off the bed but didn't say anything as he started kissing me, and I didn't mind the silence as he helped me get my clothes off. We were naked again and I was on top of him with his face smashed into the blankets a few minutes later. He moaned, he cried out, he did everything he had before, and I still enjoyed him. But I wished his hair was blonder and he looked more like Caleb.

I had to close my eyes to come, but he didn't have that problem as he made a mess of my sheets. I'd be changing them as soon as he was gone. Panting, sweaty, and not nearly as tired as I needed to be in order to get some rest so I could go to work the next morning, I tossed the condom into the trash and started up the shower in the little bathroom just off my bedroom.

This time he really was going as I heard him get his things together and head downstairs. I showered quickly, put on a pair of shorts, locked the door behind him, and then started a load of sheets before I tried to get some sleep. I didn't get much, but at least I was more rested than if I hadn't tried to get any sleep at all when I showed up for work.

My dad was already standing there with a cup of coffee in his hands and a whole lot of questions ready to go for me. "What's the

19

new man like? Will he be giving us trouble?" Dad asked as soon as I came in. He plopped a cup of coffee in front of me too, and I sniffed it gratefully. It needed to cool down some before I could actually start drinking it, but I desperately wanted to. I wasn't a morning person, not at all, and so I felt as if I were suffering just by being there so early.

"He seems fine," I said as soon as I was able to take a sip. It was still a bit too hot for me, but the caffeine would help me wake up. I just needed to stay awake long enough for the caffeine to make it into my system. I had seen a sign a few weeks back at a grocery store, not ours but somewhere in Denver where I was waiting to meet with a guy before we headed to a hotel, and it said "I Own You" with a coffee cup under it. That was pretty much how I felt every miserable morning that I had to be at the precinct. Which was really little more than a one-room office a block away from my dad's house—the same one I'd grown up in, the same one he'd probably die in. We were those kinds of people, where we lived in the same little town where he'd been born and where my grandparents had moved to when they were younger than me.

I couldn't imagine living anywhere other than Thornwood. This was home to me, and even though I went into Denver, I was always eager to come right back. There was far more to do in Denver, but I felt more alive, more whole, and more myself back home.

I hadn't had a text from the guy last night, and I didn't expect to. There had been very few guys in my life recently who hadn't gotten the picture. I needed the release, and the sex was typically good. It didn't have to mean more than that.

"He have a family coming?" Dad asked as he sat down at his desk that touched mine. Sometimes it was weird working across from my dad, but most of the time it felt completely normal. I couldn't slack like some of the guys tried to do, which was a pain sometimes when all I wanted to do was level up on whatever game I was playing on my phone that week. But I'd been coming into the station with him since Mom died, and before I had my own desk, I'd been right beside him. I'd colored at first, and after that I learned how to read, mostly from the police reports his guys turned in.

I shook my head and took a bigger sip of my coffee. It was starting to really work. "Not that I know of. He has a sister, but I don't think there's anyone else coming." I debated telling my dad that he was gay, especially since no one else was in the office yet, but I figured that wouldn't be my thing to share. I'd been outed, by my dad of all people, when I was about eight. It hadn't felt amazing to have people stare at me, or for them to tell me I couldn't possibly know my own sexuality at that age, but my dad had always been decent about it.

"Think he has any friends in town?"

I wasn't sure why my dad seemed so focused on Caleb, but I figured it was probably because nothing much happened in Thornwood. We didn't get murders, and maybe three times a year we responded to a break-in call, but that was usually just some kid coming home late and trying to be all quiet about sneaking in. Caleb moving here was kind of a big deal. If we'd had our own paper, he would have probably made the front page as not only the new guy, but a guy who had moved into the biggest house in town and bought it with a cash offer. The Smiths had told everyone who would listen about that, since it seemed so strange to them. It was a pretty big deal. I half thought Caleb must have been some kind of billionaire from Wall Street or something like that.

"I don't know, Dad. Anything happening police related?" I asked. I hoped to get the focus off Caleb, not because I didn't like him, but because it was too early in the morning for me to be thinking about having him, which was where my thoughts would probably go in a bit if my dad didn't drop him as the preferred topic for the morning.

But my dad was stubborn when he got focused on something. "You have plenty of friends. Maybe you should introduce him to one of them."

I had no idea who he would be talking about. I was friendly with the people in town, but I wouldn't actually call any of them friends. "What friends?"

Dad gave me a stern look, and if I'd been a kid, or hell, maybe a bit more awake, I would have expected to be in trouble. As it was, I was still trying to figure out these "friends" he was talking about. "Your townhouse is on my way home. I've seen the guys you bring home on occasion, and you look like you're close to them. Now, I'm not upset that I've never met any of your friends. I know you have your own life. But maybe you should introduce them to the new guy. It must be hard moving to a new town and not having anyone you know."

By the time he was done talking I was openly staring at him. "Dad...." I had no idea where to begin. "Those guys aren't my friends. We're friendly, but they're not someone I would bring over to introduce to you. And the new guy's name is Caleb."

I hoped my dad figured out what I was saying without me having to go into detail about it. I really needed him to do that for me.

"So they're...." He made a face and shook his head. "You're safe, though, aren't you? We had that discussion when you were a kid. Maybe I should have done it yearly to get it to stick."

I laughed and finished off the last of my coffee. I was finally feeling normal and awake. "Yeah, Dad. Everything's good. Now, can we please do some work? I'd really like to do something else rather than keep talking about my sex life." I tossed the coffee cup into the trash and my dad fished it out for me before tossing it into the recycling container not more than two feet behind me. He gave me another stern look, and I nodded, remembering we were supposed to be doing better as a department about that.

"Yes, anything else besides that. You go respond to the e-mails. I'll go out on patrol. The guys should start coming in at nine."

I waved to him as he gathered up his jacket and left. "See you." We all came in on a staggered schedule so someone was always around. It was a good system, I thought. And if I'd wanted to be chief someday, I would have kept it that way. But I wasn't next in line for the position, and I didn't want to be either. I liked my lack of responsibility and being given orders from my dad instead of being the one to give them and make the hard decisions. Not that those came up often, maybe once every three years, but I didn't want to be the one to fire one of my neighbors. I left that up to my dad instead. He was good at it, and at making sure the people didn't leave angry. I liked my neighbors and couldn't have imagined having to fire any of them.

I turned on my computer, grabbed a bottle of water out of the fridge while it booted up, and then opened up the e-mails. It was a lot of the usual stuff I dealt with each day. The mountain paper wanted to know if we had any news we wanted to share. Their base was three towns over, so a lot of their news was about snow and the best places to ski during the winter. I let the guy who had e-mailed the department know that we didn't have anything to share at this time.

A mom wanted to know if we could show up at her son's birthday party since he wanted to be a cop. The kid was six and his mom worked at the grocery store. I smiled thinking about how some of the older guys, those with grandkids that age, would get a kick out of doing that.

I took out my phone and texted Tony, the oldest member of our little force besides my dad. They were both in their sixties, but neither of them looked it and on my bad days they could still outshoot me.

Six year old boy wants a cop at his birthday party. Want the assignment? I texted him.

Who's his mom? Tony texted back.

I rolled my eyes. I didn't know Tony had a thing for single moms, which I knew Amy Anderson was, but I figured if it made Tony want to do it and spend time with the kid, then whatever. I brought random guys home when I didn't even know their first names, so I figured I didn't have any room to talk about love lives and relationships.

23

Amy Anderson. Works at the grocery store. Son is Tim. I texted back.

I'm in. I'll get the details from you when I get into work. Let her know I'll be there.

Thanks. I figured I knew why he said yes, and it didn't bother me in the least. Amy was pretty, I guessed. She always smiled at me and asked about my dad when I was in the grocery store. I sent the e-mail and continued on with them.

Ben, who lived two doors down from my dad, was complaining about a barking dog in the neighborhood that someone from the precinct apparently needed to deal with immediately. I shook my head at his tone, but also because I didn't remember there being any noisy dogs in the area. I was pretty sure my dad would have mentioned one to me if there had been. And besides, Ben knew who my dad was. Everyone in Thornwood did. He could have taken five minutes to walk down the street to go talk to my dad instead of spending that much time writing a pretty long and ranting e-mail about some dog barking.

I decided to call my dad and let him know.

"Hello?" he answered.

"Hey. Your neighbor Ben is complaining about a barking dog," I told him.

I heard a message come over a loudspeaker wherever he was and figured he was probably at the grocery store. "Can you get me a bag of chips while you're there? I didn't eat breakfast."

"Boy, chips aren't breakfast. I'll bring you a banana and some chocolate milk. Now, what's wrong with Ben?"

I could have argued about how I wasn't five and didn't drink chocolate milk anymore, but that was a lie. I loved everything that had chocolate in it, and my dad always got the good kind of chocolate milk for me, the one made with actual milk and not the one that had filtered water as the first ingredient. "He's complaining about a dog barking. I didn't think people had many dogs near your house. There's the golden retriever on the corner, but who else?"

"The Hendersons just rescued a few Maltese so that's probably who he's talking about. I'll stop by the hardware store to see Ben after I bring you back your breakfast. Don't skip meals. It's bad for your blood sugar or something."

I snorted. I didn't care about my blood sugar. I'd wanted to sleep in and coffee didn't do much to tide me over until lunch. We had some granola bars in a cabinet next to the computer paper, but they were nearly a year old and pretty hard at this point. "Thanks. See you in a bit."

"Bye."

I hung up and continued on with my morning of going through the e-mails.

CHAPTER THREE

Caleb

I MANAGED to get my TV set up, luckily without needing to call the cable people to help me figure out how to plug the damn wires in correctly, but after a four-hour marathon of my favorite cop show, I had Trent on my brain and needed to turn it off. He really was pretty cute. I'd never had a thing for cops, but he might have been able to convince me to change that if I was actually looking to have a relationship. Unfortunately Paul had soured me on that front. It was close to noon, I was starving, and I'd had jerky for breakfast, so I was starting to feel a bit sick to my stomach. Fortunately for me I didn't have to drive far to get to the nearest grocery store.

I grabbed a basket, figuring I'd be loading up for a while, and walked toward the frozen food section. Most of my meals came from there normally, but I did want to check out Rosie's menu completely too. Financially I was in a good place, with clients waiting for me to start working again, which I promised them would happen that week. Without a mortgage or rent payments hanging over me, I didn't see any reason not to spend a bit more on my food than I usually would have.

Six frozen pizzas went into my cart, along with a couple of local Colorado craft beers. I'd never been much for craft beer, or really trying new beers in general, but I figured I might as well give them a chance. Maybe I'd end up liking one at some point.

I grabbed some packs of cookies too. One peanut butter, a chocolate chip, and a sugar cookie were all added to my growing pile of food that wasn't going to be good for me at all. I added some double chocolate with mint chips too. I hadn't tried them, but they didn't sound disgusting, and they were cookies, so I wanted them. Without Paul there to make crappy remarks about what I ate, I wanted all the junk food I'd been limiting, or completely denying myself altogether, for the past three years.

By the time I was done, my cart looked like a frat boy's preparty haul, and I didn't feel guilty about it at all. In fact, it felt pretty good.

"Hey," the woman at the register said as I pulled into her lane. Her name tag said Amy, and there was a rose pin below it on her shirt.

"Hi." I started loading my groceries onto the belt.

"You're the new guy in town, huh?" she asked.

I nodded. "Is it that obvious?"

Amy shrugged and gave me a big smile. "We don't get a lot of new people here. I drive past your place most mornings to drop my son off at school, and I saw that your pastures are empty. When will your horses be coming in?"

I wasn't sure what the obsession was with my pastures, but I didn't think it was that weird that I didn't have any plans for them. I knew why they were all assuming I did, but my empty pastures couldn't have been the most interesting thing to happen in Thornwood that month. "I don't have any."

She looked a bit disappointed. "Oh. Well, that's okay too." She'd finished ringing up my groceries, and I paid for them. "Do you need help out?"

I shook my head. "Thanks anyway."

"Have a good day."

"You too."

After loading up my junk food haul, I headed back home, but I decided on a different route that would take me past the precinct. I thought it would have been pretty easy to find, but I was wrong about that. The only thing telling me I was near the police station was a tiny sign on the front of an office building. I would have missed it entirely except it was the only place that had two police cars parked in front. I shook my head and let the new reality of my small-town life actually start to sink in. Honestly, I kind of really liked it. It was small and adorable, which was a huge change from LA, but that was a good thing. There were no highways, no heavy traffic jams, no sirens blaring at three in the morning, no people shoving on the sidewalks. It was nice in a way I hadn't remembered LA ever being.

I drove home after that, and it didn't take me too long to bring my junk food into the house. With my groceries unloaded, I put my laptop on the island, grabbed a soda and a box of the cookies—since I didn't feel like waiting for a pizza to get done for my lunch—and got to work. I'd finished all my projects before moving, which meant a fresh start on everything. I was excited and ready to get going as I turned on my music, a nice change from the silence of the house, and got to work making a new logo for a reptile store in Arizona. They wanted a whole new setup in addition to the logo, with a new banner, new letterhead, new website—the works. It was good money for me, and I got to practice drawing a snake for their logo, which wasn't all that hard to do since it had no legs or anything really complicated about it. I thought it turned out pretty well, though, and an hour later, I had a few drafts of it sent off to them.

I checked my phone when it beeped, welcoming the distraction and at the same time praying it wasn't Paul. It was my sister, Marie, which made me really happy. *Call me if you're not busy*, her text said.

I dialed her number and waited for her to pick up, hoping it wasn't one of those times where she meant to call her at some point if I wasn't busy and not to drop everything right then and there.

"Wow, that was fast," she said as she answered.

"I had a minute between projects. How's things there?" I got off the stool, rubbed my lower back, and went to the couch to stretch out and hopefully keep my back from hurting. I was supposed to take breaks every fifteen to thirty minutes while my back recovered.

It hadn't even been a bad accident, but my doctor said I'd been hit at just the right angle to really throw things out of alignment. "Good. The boys are out working with Dan and some of his new horses. They're learning fast."

I heard the pride in my sister's voice, and it made me smile. She was a good mom, always had been. I liked kids well enough too, but I knew I wouldn't have been nearly as comfortable with them as she was. "Good. Hey, once I get things moved in here and I pick out some real furniture, why don't you all come for a visit?"

"You wouldn't mind?"

I heard the uncertainty in her voice and wondered what caused it. "Nope. Not at all. I haven't seen the boys in years. It would be good for us all to catch up." I tried to keep my voice light, since I had no idea what was going on with her and why she sounded so weird at my invitation. I hoped it wasn't anything really serious.

"Great. I'll talk it over with Dan. I think it could be fun, but I need to see what his schedule is like."

I took a second before saying anything to her just in case I said something I didn't want to. I'd meant every word of it, but my sister didn't need me nagging on her. "Or, hey, here's an idea. Why don't you and the boys come visit? Dan could get a break from them for a while." Good, I sounded perfectly light and fluffy as if my ulterior motive wasn't getting my sister and her kids away from her husband for a few weeks. I'd asked her to come to LA, but she'd always claimed the city wasn't a good place for young kids, and they couldn't afford a hotel room for a few weeks since I didn't have any place for them to stay while they were there with me. She didn't have that excuse now, though, since I doubted she could get much safer than in a tiny town like Thornwood, and I had plenty of space for them. I didn't want them moving in with me, but a few weeks would be fine.

"We'll see," Marie said. I figured that was the best I was going to get from her right then. It wasn't that I didn't like Dan; it was more that something weird had happened when she and Dan got serious. I knew she'd talk to me less. I figured on that. But she went for months without returning my calls sometimes and that had never been like her before Dan came into her life. Now I guessed her excuse was that she was busy with the kids, but a text wasn't hard to reply to, and I sent her plenty.

"So, anything fun happening there?" she asked.

I turned my head to look out at the pine trees. I had a big deck out there that I hadn't spent much time on yet. The view from my couch was plenty good for me so far. "Not really. I got groceries, so I guess that's something. Last night I thought I had an intruder."

"You okay? What happened?"

She sounded so worried, and I smiled. "Nothing much. Just some raccoons, I guess. That's what the cop I called said. Their precinct is in a little office building. I can't believe I found such a tiny town to move to."

"I can't believe you didn't move back to Kentucky when you moved out of California," she countered.

"I considered it for a little while. But I wanted to try someplace new. I've visited here, had a time-share in Colorado that I used a few times years ago, and I always thought it was pretty. No old memories, old relationships, familiar places—none of it. Colorado seemed like as good a place as any to go to."

"I guess I should just be glad you stayed in the US," she grumbled. "I wish you were closer, though. I miss you, and I think the boys would like to see you more."

"You can fly out whenever you want. I'll cover the airfare, and you can all stay here. I've got plenty of room." I wanted her to take me up on my offer but figured she probably wouldn't for a while yet—though I did plan to see her at some point, even if I had to go to Kentucky to get that. She was my sister, and I hadn't seen her in years. It wasn't right, and I wanted to see her more. I didn't know for sure, but I had a pretty good idea Dan was the reason I hadn't seen her recently, and that upset me. We'd always been close so that was the only thing I could point to as being different.

"I'll talk to Dan, and we'll figure something out," Marie told me. It was better than nothing I guessed, so I didn't push her anymore on it. "Ben wants to talk to you if you have a minute."

I shrugged, not knowing what my youngest nephew would want but figuring I had some time to talk to him anyway. "Sure. Put him on."

"Great. He's right here." There was some shuffling of the phone, and I waited for him to come on.

"Uncle Caleb?"

"Hey, kiddo," I said. Ben was ten, and likely my favorite of my nephews, though that was probably because he was the only one who seemed fairly normal to me. The middle kid, Robbie, was sometimes a bit loud for my tastes. The oldest, Daniel, was all about showing horses, mostly in western pleasure, and competing with his horse and being the best at everything he did. It was great for him to be so driven, but it was a bit much for me at times. I only talked to them every few months or so, but I did get e-mails. When we were little, my sister never talked about wanting kids or being a mom, but she seemed to like it a lot now.

"Mom said you got a bunch of land and horse stalls," Ben said.

I wasn't sure why everyone seemed so fixated on my land. Maybe I should have been renting it out to these people so they could get over their curiosity. "Yep. I got some pastures with the house," I told him vaguely.

"Um. Could I maybe have a horse there? Dad won't get me one yet. And you don't have any horses, do you? I'd just want one."

"Ben!" I heard Marie hiss at him just before there was more fumbling with the phone and my sister came back on the phone. "Caleb, I'm sorry. I didn't know he was going to ask for a horse. That's completely unreasonable of him. I'll have a talk with him about that."

I didn't really think it'd been a big deal but whatever. "It didn't bother me any. If he was closer and I didn't have to take care of the horse, I would have given him one. I've got the land

and the pastures and stalls. I'm just not much of a horse person. I know what I'm doing, but I'm not all wrapped up in them like your kids are."

She seemed a little calmer as she chuckled and said, "I guess one of us had to grow out of it. Shame, though. You were always a natural at riding."

"That's what our neighbor said when we were growing up. I just liked showing off." I remembered feeling invincible when I'd be kneeling on the back of a horse while it was galloping. Playing around like that had been a highlight of my childhood. Somehow I doubted Dan let the kids goof off like that. He seemed far more serious about riding than the neighbor who had taught Marie and me to ride had been. Maybe that was a good thing, though. I remembered all the broken bones and sprains I'd had growing up whenever I'd fallen off.

"You were good at it." I didn't argue with her. "Well, I guess I'll let you get back to your day."

I didn't want to let her go so soon, but I couldn't think of anything to say that would keep my sister on the phone with me. "Hey, Marie, is everything okay there?" I finally asked.

"Of course. Why wouldn't it be?"

I didn't really have an answer for her. Something just felt off, but I was states away from her and hadn't seen her in years, with no explanation really of why I couldn't go to the house or they couldn't come visit me. "Nothing. No worries. It's not a big deal. Send me some pics of the kids please? I've got some room on the bookshelf, and I could use some more family photos."

"Sure. I'll e-mail you some tonight. Have fun out there."

"You too. Bye."

She hung up, and I sighed as I turned onto my side to look out at the pine trees. There was something going on; I was sure of it. But I couldn't say exactly what it was, and in the end I figured I just had to trust my sister to take care of herself and the kids. I had no basis for not liking Dan. I didn't even really know him all that well. But something about him made me wonder what his deal was. I don't know. Maybe I was going crazy.

I got up from the couch and went back over to my computer. There was plenty of work to do, and the first e-mail I opened made me groan. It was from a repeat client, one who hadn't finished paying his last bill, and he expected me to start work immediately on a new project for him.

> *Mr. Sumson,*
> *As much as I would enjoy helping you with*
> *your new website and business endeavor, I cannot*
> *begin work on it until you have finished paying my*
> *last invoice. Additionally, because of the overdue*
> *status of your last project, if I was to do this website*
> *for you I would need half of my fee up front instead*
> *of my usual 25 percent.*
> *Caleb Robinson*

There. That should get his attention. It wasn't as if I was singling him out to be mean to, though he would likely feel that I was. He could be a bit temperamental and was one of the clients I hadn't enjoyed spending time with in person while in LA. I preferred e-mail and texts for all things, but some clients had insisted on doing face-to-face meetings. Lucky for me, though, now that I was in the middle of nowhere in Colorado, I didn't have to have meetings with people anymore. Besides, where was I going to have them? On my kitchen island while I drank beer with my clients? That wouldn't be very professional of me. But then again, I'd been a fuck toy for my boss, and had often given him pleasure in his office during working hours, so what did I honestly know about being professional?

Thinking about Paul, and how upset his wife had been when she'd found out, made me restless. I got up and walked around with a cookie in one hand and my beer in the other. While we'd been having sex I hadn't really ever thought about her or how much Paul's cheating would have hurt her. Now I knew he'd been cheating on a lot of people, and part of me felt sick since I'd thought I loved him. I just felt bad for his wife, and I wondered if she knew what kind of a man she'd married. He'd always promised me she did, that it was just part of their relationship, and things were fine. That had been his tune, up until I'd threatened to tell her after one of our fights. I hadn't been strong enough to walk away, though, and in the end she figured things out for herself. She was still with him for some reason. Probably because he'd spun it so that it was my fault: I'd seduced him. I was the evil one.

I rolled my eyes and took another cookie. If she decided to stick it out with him, that was her problem, not mine. I was completely done with that situation. I wanted to do something, to get out of the house for a while and away from my work. I had to send out one quick e-mail, letting a new client know I needed some more information about what they were looking for before I could officially start on their brand relaunch, but after that I grabbed up my jacket, and walked down the trail that led from my house toward the barn.

The previous owners—the Smiths I guessed their name was, though I really hadn't paid much attention to anything about the house after I'd fallen in love with the view—had raised horses on the property. The barn was recently updated from what I could tell. I didn't know much about barns at all, but maybe I should have considered leasing out the horse farm part of the property. I shook my head, instantly disliking that idea. I didn't want strangers around my house. I'd had enough of people I didn't know near me in LA. I didn't need that here too. Plus, the owners of the farm down the road said they boarded horses. I didn't want to make enemies of them by competing with their business without meaning to.

The Smiths had left some tools and I took a rake and cleaned out some of the bedding left in a stall of the barn. It wasn't soiled, more like forgotten in a corner, and within minutes I had the barn cleaned out. Maybe it was a shame not to have horses in there. It was a good property and already set up to handle probably twenty horses at full capacity. Before the car accident, or nonaccident, I might have considered getting a horse to put in this barn. But with my back hurting and sometimes going out, I couldn't guarantee that I'd always be able to care for a horse of my own.

I shrugged it off and went out, stopping at the barn's entrance when I saw a cop car in my driveway. I walked up the trail to meet Trent, who was getting out of his car. "Hey," I said once I reached him.

"Hi." He took off his hat and brushed his hand through his hair—still the color of my dark chocolate collection, which I had managed to unpack finally—and it was maybe an inch shorter than mine. I wanted to touch it like he was, but I stopped myself from reaching out and doing just that. "What are you doing here?" That sounded a bit rude, so I added, "Not that I mind the company. I'm just not used to seeing a cop so often without there being an issue. I'm not in trouble, am I?"

He smiled at me, and my heart did the little pitter-patter crap it sometimes did when a guy gave me the kind of sexy grin Trent was giving me. I really needed to get myself under control. He was hot. I could appreciate that, but I wasn't in the market for a relationship. I'd have to content myself with just checking him out.

"Do you want to be in trouble?" he asked. I rolled my eyes in hopes of distracting him from my blush. At least it was pretty dark out. "I wanted to let you know you should keep the lights around your house, the garage, and the barn on at night, or at least get the kind that turn on when there's movement," he told me when I didn't say anything for a moment.

The garage made sense to me, and even though I didn't have horses in the barn, I guessed I could see the benefit of that too. I was planning on getting a security system installed at some point too, so I'd just do it all at the same time. "They aren't working right now. I need to get an electrician out here. You could have called and told me that, though. You didn't have to drive all the way out here." I leaned against my SUV, and he propped himself up against his car.

"It's not like it's all that far of a drive. I was out on patrol anyway."

I nodded, because that was pretty reasonable.

"And maybe I just wanted to see you again," he tacked on, making me purse my lips.

I shook my head. "Let me stop you right there. Trent, you're nice and all, but I can't do that."

He didn't look like my words had really fazed him all that much. "Do what?"

I shrugged, not really sure how to explain everything I couldn't do with him. "A relationship." That was the start of it. I couldn't give in, couldn't see where it would go. I wasn't up to dealing with another guy, and I'd only been away from Paul for two months. It sucked that I couldn't just give in and enjoy Trent as I so clearly wanted to, but that's just how it was.

Now he looked a bit disappointed. "Are you with someone right now?" he asked, as if that could be the only possible reason for me to say no to him.

I shook my head. "Definitely not. But I did just end things, and it was a bit messy." That was an understatement, and I really wasn't up to going into it with him while standing on my driveway. I took a deep breath. "But if you want to be friends, I would love to have a friend here."

He nodded slowly. "Okay. I can do friends too."

"Great." It wasn't great at all. Instead I felt like I'd just hurt him. Relationships were complicated, and I thought I tended to have ones that seemed more complicated than most people's. "So I'll see you later?"

"Yeah. See you." He got back into his car, and I stood there wishing I could have just said yes to whatever he'd been offering. But two months was not long enough to get over someone and start something new, so I let him go and headed back inside to my TV, my attention-hungry clients, and the box of cookies I'd call dinner.

CHAPTER FOUR

Trent

BEING TURNED down wasn't really something new to me, but it still stung to have Caleb tell me no. Problem was, I hadn't actually been asking him for a relationship, or anything serious really. All I'd been interested in was getting him into bed, which normally wasn't a problem for me. I pulled into Rosie's parking lot, then noticed I'd missed a call. Who it was from, though, made my breath catch in my chest.

It took me a good five minutes to calm down enough to be able to call her back and sound normal while doing it. "Hi, Laura," I said when she picked up the phone.

"Hi, Trent. How are you?"

There was really no good way of telling my partner's mom how I was doing. "I'm okay. Are things good with you?"

"Yes. More or less. Simon's birthday is coming up next month."

I nodded. I didn't need the reminder. His birthday passed every year, and each year the man I loved, the one I'd thought I'd spend my life with, got a little older even when he never moved a muscle. "He'll be thirty-seven," I said, letting her know I was well aware that his birthday was coming up, and also that I hadn't forgotten anything else about him.

"Right. Thirty-seven. So young." She sniffled, and I heard her mumble something.

"What's wrong?" I asked her, my heartbeat picking up. Laura and I didn't talk. It was too hard—for both of us. Her calling me meant something was very wrong, and I needed to know what it was right away.

She still sounded like she was trying not to cry when she came back to the phone. "We'll be turning off the machines at six o'clock on his birthday. I'd like you to be there. If you want to be." And then I understood why she was so upset, and I felt like I couldn't breathe again. It was the accident, seeing Simon lying there broken at the bottom of a mountain, hearing that he'd never be able to wake up—all of it was there and it was all new again.

"Trent? Trent, honey? Are you okay?"

"No...," I squeaked out. I wasn't okay. That was on a completely different planet than where I was right then. I forced myself to take one breath, and then another. I licked my lips and touched my face, realizing that I'd been crying. "I'll come," I finally managed. "Will Cassandra be okay with me being there, though? I don't want to make trouble for you and your family."

Simon's little sister, Cassandra, had never figured out how to forgive me for an accident that wasn't my fault. I didn't blame her, though. If her brother hadn't met me, if we'd never fallen in love, then he might have been okay.

"She'll have to be. You loved him," Laura told me.

"I still love him," I said, perhaps a little more sharply than I should have. My feelings for Simon, the man I'd lost, had never changed. But his family didn't know I'd said good-bye to my Simon a long time ago. It'd been five years, and he would have never wanted to be kept alive on life support that long. I hadn't said any of that to Laura, though. I'd never felt like it was my place to tell her that. I'd loved Simon. He'd been my partner, but he'd been their son, and we'd been together less than a year. I hadn't known how to tell her that her choice of prolonging his life when the doctors had told us there was nothing they could do wasn't right, and eventually, as time passed, I realized nothing I could have said would have changed their minds.

"So we'll see you next month?" she asked.

I nodded. "I'll see you there."

"Okay. Bye, Trent."

"Thank you for calling me, Laura."

She was getting ready to start crying again. "Of course."

We hung up, and I sat there in my car in front of my mom's restaurant for a good ten minutes before I got out and walked inside. I was greeted with smiles, a hug from Roxanne, a waitress, and a wave from some of the guys before being put into a booth.

"What can I get you, hon?" Roxanne asked. She'd been a friend of my mom's and was as much a part of the diner as my mom had been. They'd even named their kids after the same letters. Her kid was Thomas, and I figured he had to be in high school by now.

"Cookie shake and a double burger please," I told her. I didn't want to talk to anyone, not really, but I had to give her my order since I didn't have a "usual," and besides, if I acted off, people would start asking me what was wrong, and I couldn't have handled that.

"You got it, punkin." She wrote it down, then gave me a little wink. The nicknames I had in this town, mostly because they'd all seen me grow up as the chief's kid, sometimes bordered on ridiculous. Other times they annoyed me. Roxie could call me whatever she wanted, though. I'd put up with it from her, because after my mom died she stepped in sometimes. The guys on the force, plus the people in Rosie's, had really raised me during the rough patches after her death, when my dad was having trouble. I'd done my homework in a booth with a strawberry milkshake, and got rides to school in patrol cars when my dad was too depressed to do much more than say hi to me.

It hadn't always been hard, but now, after what had happened to Simon, I could see a little of what he'd been through with me. I'd been really young when Mom died, but for years afterward Dad had rough patches where it was like she died all over again and he was just beginning to grieve. Even now it happened occasionally, and I wondered if I'd feel the same at times too, once Simon was really gone. He'd felt gone to me for five years, though. I hadn't moved on, not at all, but I didn't have relationships anymore either. I had sex, a lot of it, but I didn't let my heart or my emotions get involved. If they didn't want me, so what? If I didn't want them, that was no big deal either.

I looked up to see Caleb sitting down across from me and forced my thoughts away from Simon so Caleb couldn't see that I was upset. I'd known him for about two days now, and I was pretty sure even people who knew me wouldn't be able to tell something was off, so it was unlikely Caleb could. But I wanted to be careful just in case.

"Hey. Decide that you needed to eat?" I asked.

Caleb smiled at me and I smiled back. It was easy pretending everything was fine.

"Yeah. I finished a package of cookies and realized I needed to eat more than that for dinner."

I laughed, and I was glad it sounded natural. "Well, here is definitely better than cookies. I can promise you that."

He started looking through the menu, and I watched him. "What do you do?" I asked after a few minutes.

"Graphic design. How are the chicken tenders?"

I wasn't going to say my mom's food wasn't good, so him asking was kind of a moot point. "They're nice." Roxie brought out a basket of fries for me and a side plate for me to put the ketchup on so I didn't get it all over my fries.

"What'll you be having, Trent's friend?" she asked.

"Roxie, this is Caleb," I said. "He just bought Rocky Creek Stables."

He put the menu down. "Hey. Iced tea and chicken tenders please."

"You got it." The menus stayed on the table, and she went to put his order in while I started on my fries. I pushed them toward him so he could have some too, which he did, so I was glad Roxie would bring out as many baskets as I could eat. I'd need all the fried, salty comfort food I could get that night.

"Rocky Creek Stables?" Caleb asked as he finished one fry and reached for another.

I nodded and thought it was weird he didn't know what the place he bought had been called. "When I was a kid it was a touristy place. Your property backs to government land so the Smiths used to take people through there on the trails. It was kind of a big deal when they stopped the rental business since, as kids, we used to go onto their property and feed the horses. My first job, when I was fifteen, was cleaning out stalls there until I was old enough to lead some of the rides."

"Huh. No wonder everyone seems so intent on me getting horses back out there. Even my youngest nephew asked me today if I could buy him a horse and keep it on my property." Caleb shook his head, then wiped his hands on his jeans.

"How many nephews do you have?" I asked.

He pulled out his phone and slid his finger across a few times before handing it to me. I looked down at a picture of the same pretty woman who was up on his bookshelf. Only this time she was older and had three little kids with her. The biggest one was almost as tall as her. "That's my sister, Marie, and her three kids. The shortest is Ben, Robbie is the one in the middle with the red hair, and Daniel is the one that's nearly scowling beside her. He's fourteen."

Caleb rolled his eyes, and I smiled. "Cute kids. I can see some horses in the background."

He nodded and took his phone back. "Yeah. They show them. Mostly in western pleasure. Sequined shirts, black leather chaps, saddles with lots of silver on them." He shrugged, and I wondered why he didn't seem to like horses at all. Sure, some people just didn't like them. But I wasn't one of them, and he had all that land....

"But you don't?"

Caleb made a face. "Show horses? No. Not at all. I can ride, but I don't show. It's not something I've ever been interested in. Her kids seem to like it, though, so that's great for them."

"But you do like horses?" I asked.

He shrugged. "Yeah. I do. I guess. I mean, riding is fun and they're beautiful animals."

"Then why not have some?" I might have been pressuring him, or being a pest, or whatever else. But he had all that land, and it was already set up for horses. And he liked them. He'd just said that. From his house and knowing that he'd paid for it in cash, I knew his reasons weren't that he couldn't afford them.

Our food came before he had a chance to answer me. Then for a while there, we just ate, making soft noises as we enjoyed the food. I was drinking my milkshake when he made the first little moan that sounded so much like a sex noise, I nearly choked on my shake.

"Sorry," I said, coughing. "Went down the wrong pipe." It hadn't, but I didn't want him to know the real reason I'd had an issue with my straw.

"This is really good food," he said as he finished off his meal.

I nodded. I knew it was. I was halfway through both my burger and my shake and mostly done with the basket of fries. I didn't know if I'd be ordering more or what my plans were for the rest of the night. I didn't want to go home, though. Not just yet at least. Simon hadn't ever been in that townhouse, so it wasn't that.

It was more like I didn't want to just sit at home thinking about him. But getting on the dating app and finding some random person to take to a hotel didn't really work for me that night either. Most nights I would have been fine with that. I liked hooking up. I liked the lack of complications and how there weren't any expectations. I never saw them again and even if they did text me and ask me for another night, I always said no. I let them know it had nothing to do with them, but I didn't do repeat visits. I was an ass, and I'd been called worse than that often enough. But really, these guys were on a hookup app. What did they expect? A ring, a key to my townhouse, and permission to get a dog after one good fuck? Not likely. I didn't ignore their texts or play other games like that, but I didn't do begging either. Some guys had to be shut down hard or else they wouldn't get the hint that I wasn't interested in them for anything more than a one-night stand. That didn't make me evil; it made me uncomplicated.

"I can't take care of a horse. I had a car accident and sometimes my back acts up," Caleb told me, bringing me back to our earlier conversation. "If I had someone that could take care of it, I might have one, but then it would be more their horse than mine. I didn't mean to buy a horse property. I just wanted the biggest house I could afford in a tiny town."

"Why Thornwood?" I asked. No one really moved to my town. Plenty of people moved out, usually to go to college in Denver or northern Colorado near Fort Collins. But very rarely did people choose to move to Thornwood. It was weird.

He smiled and pushed away his empty plate. "Honestly? I took out a map of the US, closed my eyes, and picked a state. Then once I'd decided on Colorado, I did the same thing with a big map of Colorado. My finger landed on Thornwood, and I called a real estate agent that worked in the area."

I stared at him. "You seriously decided to move here because your finger landed on our town?"

Caleb gave me a little laugh and nodded. He was blushing again, and I shook my head, not believing what I was hearing. "Sounds crazy, I'm sure."

"Yeah, just a bit," I agreed with him.

"But I can work from anywhere, and once I walked in and saw those big windows in the living room, I fell in love. So I bought the house, moved in, and now at some point I need to go buy a lot of furniture because I moved from a one-bedroom apartment to this huge house, and it feels so empty."

I was still shaking my head at him. "Wow. That's just... okay, then. You've got to be the craziest rich person I've ever met."

Caleb looked a little surprised at my assumption. "I'm not that rich. I got a good settlement for the accident, but I still have to work."

That was a little better, I guessed. But I was still really shocked at what he'd done.

"Do you want to come over?" he asked.

I frowned as I wondered what he could be getting at. "I thought you didn't want...." I looked around the diner as I let my voice trail off. People there knew I was gay, because it wasn't like my sexuality had ever really been a secret, but at the same time, I didn't want them knowing I was into casual sex either.

He held up one of his hands, stopping me. "I don't. I just figured we could watch a movie, have a beer, eat some cookies. As friends."

I relaxed a little because I'd been wrong and my earlier thoughts were right. Caleb wasn't interested, which was fine. I was still interested in him, but I could handle rejection and besides, friends were always good to have. "Sure. A movie sounds good."

We were done with dinner, so I put some cash down on the table and started to get up.

"You don't have to do that," Caleb told me.

I shrugged, because paying for dinner didn't really bother me. "It's fine. I'll meet you back at your house, then?"

"Sure." I followed him out, waved to Roxie, and then watched him get in his SUV before I got into my patrol car. He really needed to get those tags looked at, and I figured I'd mention it at some point, but no one in Thornwood would give him a ticket for that. We didn't really give tickets. We talked to parents, gave hard lectures on speeding, but unless someone was actually being reckless, no one on the force gave tickets to the people in town, and if it warranted a ticket, it usually meant we'd be taking them to jail too. Which was a pretty long and fairly boring drive to the nearest big town with holding cells. We didn't have any in Thornwood.

Getting to his house from the diner took less than five minutes, about the same amount of time it took to get anywhere in town. It was pretty late, so I went slower to watch out for any deer that might cross the road. Most people took it slow, but every once in a while we got some people who enjoyed speeding through our little town. The people who got lost on their way to gambling up at Black Hawk and Central City and ended up zooming through town were some of my favorite tickets to write. People rarely considered the road to be residential, but the truth was there were plenty of kids in town who played by the streets or tossed balls across the road to each other, even after I'd told them not to a dozen times before.

I parked next to Caleb's SUV and stretched my legs to catch up to him as he walked up the steps. A movie sounded good and would probably give me the distraction I needed tonight. I hoped so anyway.

Half an hour later, I was restless, and though the movie was supposedly a pretty good one, I could barely focus on it. I curled my fingers over my knee and tried to force myself to relax. Maybe getting a guy in Denver wouldn't be such a bad thing. At least then I could exhaust myself with someone. I didn't want to do that, especially tonight while my thoughts circled around Simon, but I didn't know what else to do in order to get my racing heart under control. I felt caged, like I needed to stretch out or go for a run or... just something to get myself back under control.

"You okay?" Caleb asked a few minutes after I'd made the decision to leave but hadn't yet figured out a polite way to excuse myself.

I started to nod, then finished off by shaking my head. "Not really. Look, I'm sorry I came over. I'm not in a good space right now. I should probably go."

He looked disappointed as his expression, one of mild curiosity, turned into a frown. He nodded, though, and I got up from the couch. "Okay. See you later?"

"Of course." I was at the door, and I should have just opened it and gone right back outside. But... I ran my hands through my hair. I was too messed up for this, for friends, for hanging out. Caleb was nice, and as a friend he could have been great. But I didn't need a friend right then. I needed someone to screw and never have to look at again. I needed someone who would let me treat them like a sex toy to vent my frustration about what had happened to Simon, about losing the only person I'd loved. And even if the accident hadn't been my fault, in my mind I could hear Cassandra screaming at me the way she'd done that first night in the hospital. It was all my fault because I'd fallen in love with Simon and he'd fallen in love with me and if he hadn't, then her big brother would still be around for her. She was wrong, but she was so right too.

Caleb put his arms around me, and once again I realized I'd been crying. "I'm not good company right now," I told him, as if that weren't completely obvious by the way I was crying and shaking.

He nodded and released me. I thought he was letting me go to deal with my problems in the only way I really knew how to: naked on top of someone else. But he took my hand and pulled me back to the couch. I sat after his gentle shove to my stomach. I could have stopped him, could have just moved out of the way and left like I should have. But restlessness warred with frustration within me and so much of me just wanted to stay. I liked Caleb. It wasn't just that he was the only gay guy I knew of in Thornwood. It was that he smiled, and I felt like smiling too—even now when I didn't really want to. He put one of his knees on the couch beside my hip, and I looked up at him. I didn't know what his plan was, and part of me was scared.

"What were you asking me for this afternoon?" His voice was quiet. He'd turned off the movie when I stood up, since the TV behind him was now completely black.

I licked my lips and weighed my options. I didn't want a relationship, couldn't handle one even on my best days, and he'd said no to one. The easy way out of there would have been to tell him I wanted to be serious with him. I could scare him by saying I wanted to move in. After two days of knowing me, that would probably make anyone run for their lives. But I didn't want to shut him down like the persistent guys on my app. I still wanted him to be around, and so I simply shook my head and left my hands on the couch, even though I wanted to touch him.

"Sex," I replied simply. I watched him, judging his reaction for myself. He pulled his leg off the couch, but he didn't go far as he sat down next to me, facing me, with one leg pulled up under him. It wasn't a rejection, not really, but it wasn't the reaction I was expecting either. I'd figured him for the kind of guy who would have turned me down flat. He didn't come across at all like one of the guys I toyed with. I chose needy, easily controlled men who let me fuck them and then leave them. If I misjudged them and they turned out to be a bit more clingy than I'd anticipated, it was usually easy to get rid of them.

He was built for sex with a great body, but he didn't move as if he was looking for his next dick and he didn't talk like it either. He seemed like all he wanted was a friend, and I couldn't be that for him right now. Maybe the next day. After all it wasn't as if either of us was going away anytime soon, but tonight I couldn't be a friend, not when all I wanted was to forget myself with someone else. And I wasn't asshole enough to do that to someone I wanted to be friends with. So I tried to get up again, but he wrapped his fingers around my wrist.

"I'm no good right now," I told him as I covered his hand with my own. I'd pry his fingers off my wrist if I needed to. It wouldn't even take much, just me putting my fingers around his thumb and manipulating his hand off of me. His hand would go wherever I moved his thumb. I knew that. But I didn't do that, and I didn't make myself stand up. I was a coward and a horrible person. That's all I could think to explain why I sat there and let him straddle me. He bent down and kissed me. His mouth was soft and his kiss gentle, like he was scared of something. I kissed him back, but I was a lot rougher. And I put one of my hands behind his head, right on his neck, so he couldn't pull away. I was hard, because I'd been so worked up and still was, but having him on my lap with his thickening cock pressing against my stomach through his jeans and the thick material of my uniform made it even more impossible for me to do what was right.

Caleb found the fly of my pants and pressed his palm against me. I jerked back, because he surprised me, but it didn't take me long to settle down and let him rub and squeeze me through my uniform. This wasn't right; I didn't mess around with guys in my uniform. And I didn't want to lose Caleb as the good friend he could very easily be. But he opened my pants, pushed my briefs aside, and found my cock. I opened my mouth and shot my tongue between his teeth. I should have let him go. I should have pushed him off me and told him that tonight just wasn't going to work. But he was hot, ready, and wanting me. And I was weak for letting him.

He was good with his hand, but a hand job wouldn't have fixed my problems tonight, so I reached to the button of his jeans and took him out. He was nearly fully hard and already a bit wet on his tip. I rubbed his head and stroked his length until he was panting and shaking against my chest. I didn't know if he had a bed already set up in the house, but really it didn't matter. Sex was just as easy on the couch. Hell, his kitchen island would have worked just fine too. I pulled my wallet out of my pocket and was glad I'd left my holster and gun locked up in the car. It was one less thing to get in the way.

If he noticed me pull a condom out of my wallet, he didn't mention it. He could think whatever he wanted. I wasn't being responsible with our budding friendship, but I could be safe with both of us. And, I reasoned as I moved him off me and got behind him on the couch, sex took two people. I wasn't solely responsible for what we were doing.

CHAPTER FIVE

Caleb

MY JEANS slipped down a little on my hips when he moved me over on the couch and got behind me. My heart raced and really, I didn't know what had made me decide to do this. Trent had looked so miserable sitting beside me on the couch, like he needed to be anywhere but here. I hadn't been ready to let him go, but sex wasn't a good way to keep someone next to me. I dug my fingers into the seat cushion of my couch at the first touch of Trent's tongue against my asshole. I'd been rimmed before, plenty of times, but with him it felt different. Maybe because I wasn't fully into it, maybe because I'd only known him for two days, but I knew I should have stopped this.

"Trent, stop," I said. And instantly I felt guilty for not having sex with him because I'd started everything. He'd said he needed to go, plenty of times, but I kept pushing, and it was on the tip of my tongue to say never mind and just have sex with him anyway. He was gorgeous, and I was sure I'd enjoy it. But I wasn't into the random, casual sex he seemed to want from me, and I was already pretty disgusted with myself after my relationship with Paul.

Trent pulled away, and once his hands were no longer on my hips, I got up and fixed my jeans. He looked confused, and I thought again of how easy it would be to simply say yes to him, that I'd made a mistake, that everything was fine. But it wasn't.

"I can't do this. Not tonight," I told him as he stood up too and adjusted his clothes. He was still hard, and I was quickly losing

49

my erection. Fucking perfect. I wanted to sigh and knock my head against the wall a few dozen times.

He nodded and started heading for the door. "I get it."

"Where are you going?" I asked. I thought maybe we could watch the rest of the movie, each of us have another beer, and pretend this hadn't happened.

But he kept walking to my door. "I'm not in the right space for a movie and hanging out right now. You don't know this about me, and most people don't actually, but when I'm not okay, like now, the only thing I've found that calms me down is sex. So I'm going to go fix myself."

"You're with someone?" I asked, feeling a bit sick to my stomach all over again. Not this. I couldn't be the other person another time.

He shook his head. "It's not like that. I'll talk to you later. Bye."

It took me longer than it should have to figure out what he meant, but after he left, I finally understood and had to sit down on my couch.

I realized Trent hadn't needed to have sex with me; I was merely convenient. He could have had sex with anyone and probably would while I sat here staring at a black TV screen. I shook my head, got up, and downed half a bottle of beer before I stopped being mad at him, and at myself. Because, really, if I was going to actually look at the situation and be honest about it, I'd nearly had sex with a man I'd known for two days. That might have been what Trent did, and I suspected it was, but I wasn't like that. And I'd pushed him into staying and into having sex.

I wasn't going to say no to being friends with him, but sex was most definitely off the table between us now. And yet, as I stood there leaning over my island and alternating between bites of a cookie and sips of my beer, I couldn't stop thinking about how much I'd wanted him. It was weird and definitely not something I should have been thinking about while he probably had his dick in someone else. But the thought was there anyway.

I groaned and pulled out my phone. It was still kind of early in California, and my only close friend, Dean, would still be up. I was sure of it.

The phone rang in my hand, and I thought maybe he'd gone to bed early. Or that he and his wife were out doing something much more fun than I was. But then he picked up, and I felt instantly better at having my friend to talk to.

"Hey, Caleb."

"Hi. How's things there?" I asked. I wasn't calling him to get advice on the Trent situation. We weren't like that, and I didn't go running to people when I had a problem. I hadn't even told him I'd been with Paul until last year when I'd tried unsuccessfully to leave him. But it just felt good to talk to someone about nothing at all for a while.

He chuckled. "Oh, you know. Backed-up highways, all those people with their hybrids everywhere, can't find a decent greasy burger between all the health food places."

I smiled, remembering, and took my mostly empty beer and the box of nearly gone cookies over to the couch where I lay down and snacked.

"Sounds miserable."

"It is. How's mountain living and no traffic, then?"

"Pretty good, actually." When I wasn't making ridiculous mistakes and nearly having sex with a guy I wanted but had barely even started to get to know.

"Dean, you tell him about Sam," I heard Dean's wife, Natalie, call to him.

"Woman, I'm getting to that!"

"Get faster!"

I laughed. "So what's going on with Sam?"

"He got beat up at school today." I heard the anger in Dean's voice, and I was right there with him.

"What? How? Why?" I adored Sam, even more than my own nephews, though he was about their age. But I'd watched Sam grow

51

up. I'd given him swimming lessons as a kid and had babysat him for years.

"Because he decided to come out in his English class."

For a moment there I didn't know what to say. "I thought he was going to keep that under wraps for a while." It hadn't been my decision, but I hadn't been against it either. Kids were cruel more often than not, and he'd already been tormented pretty often for being black, and now they were going to beat up on him for being gay? Damn. Poor kid. I shook my head just thinking about it.

"That was what we'd talked about. But he had to write an essay about one thing that's special about him and he wrote it and the teacher I guess liked it so much that she had him read it in front of the class. Sam says she let him decide if he wanted to or not but my guess is he was just so damn proud of his A that he decided to go for it." Dean groaned, and I could hear the frustration in his voice. "I just wanted to keep him safe. You know? I love him, Nat loves him, and we'll always accept him. He can be completely open and out with us at home. But I wanted him to lay low for a little while in that school."

"So what are you doing now?" I asked. I could understand Dean's frustration. Having kids was hard, which was probably why I didn't have any. That and the whole not having someone to raise them with part since I was not interested in being a single parent from the start. Although I did know there was a possibility of that happening later on.

"Nat wants to pull him out of school and homeschool him for a while. I'm not opposed to it. When he was getting teased, we talked about it some and decided that it would be okay once he grew up a bit. But he's got loads of bruises right now, and I want to go beat up some kids for hurting my little man."

"I've got plenty of room, you know, if you wanted to come spend some time out here and get him away from all of that for a while." I had just extended the same offer to my sister and her kids, but I highly doubted she'd take me up on it. And from the sound of things there, Sam needed a bit of time away from his life in LA and all the crappy people in it.

Dean didn't say anything at first. "You sure about that? You did just move there. Maybe you want some time to relax, move your stuff in, get the lay of the land so to speak."

I laughed at that and put my now-empty beer bottle down on the floor next to me. I had three cookies left though, and knew they wouldn't last much longer. I should have grabbed some real groceries at the store, but junk food was kind of what I ran on most days. "Dean, seriously, my stuff is moved in. The town has one street and about ten stores in it. Come on out if you can get away. If you can't and want to send Sam out alone, that would be fine too. I'll take him fishing or something."

"You'd go fishing?"

I made a face. "Yeah. Probably not. So I'd make sure he ate something more than chips and cookies." Unlike myself most days. "And didn't get lost in the woods."

"I'll talk to Nat about it. Some time away might do us all some good."

I nodded and figured Nat would probably agree with me and want to come out. She always did like me. I couldn't wait for her to make some of her fresh pecan pie for me again. Thinking about it right now, I knew I'd be deprived if she never sent me any again. "How's the job hunt going?" I asked as I munched on a cookie.

Dean sighed, and I heard him get up from wherever he was sitting. Probably from his dark green recliner that was even older than the sofa I was currently stretched out over but twice as comfortable too. "It's.... Well, there aren't many jobs for a general contractor here right now. I'm still looking, though."

I knew he was trying to be optimistic, but I heard the disappointment in his voice too. "I'm sorry."

"Don't be. I'm going to go talk over a trip with Nat so I'll call you later."

"Sure. Bye, Dean."

"Later."

I hung up and rested the phone on my stomach as I finished off the last of the cookies. Times were hard for Dean, especially since his income was all they had. I'd offered to help them a lot of times since the settlement money had come in, but he'd always refused me flat out. I wished there was more I could do for them.

I got up from the couch and went back to the island after tossing out my trash. It was time for me to order a whole lot of furniture to fill up my new house.

I DIDN'T see or hear from Trent for three days, but that was most likely because I'd been so busy with people delivering furniture that I hadn't been to Rosie's, or anywhere in town, during that time. But even when I did see him, it was just a video of him and a lot of other cops rescuing some horses from a neglectful farm south of Denver.

I decided to leave the guys putting my bed together alone and give him a call just to say hi. And I was also a bit curious about why a Thornwood cop would be needed for something that far away. "Hey, it's Caleb," I said when he answered the phone.

"Hi. How're you doing?"

I shrugged. I'd thought about him a lot over the past few days, mostly wondering how he was, and who he was having sex with. But I tried not to think about that while I was on the phone with him right then. I'd already spent plenty of time imagining who he could have run to after I turned him down the other night.

"Good. I saw you on TV rescuing some horses." I headed downstairs and took some pain pills because my back was acting up after I'd attempted to help put a dresser together before the furniture guys took over. Now I just needed my couch, a glass of water, and some mindless TV to keep me company for a few hours until they got done putting my house together for me since I was useless in that department.

"How'd I look?" Trent asked.

I smiled at his ego. "Covered in mud and tired but still hot." There was no use in pretending I didn't find him attractive after what we'd done. "Why'd they call you guys down? Doesn't Parker have its own police force?"

"Yeah, but it was sort of an 'all available guys come help out' situation. One of my buddies in Denver called me up and told me about it. I was off, so I headed down there to do what I could. A place called Green Acres Equine Sanctuary took them in if you want to check the horses out."

I made a face at the name. "Why would I want to do that?"

"In case you ever want to adopt. The woman who runs it is Evaline Green." He chuckled, and I wished he was there with me instead of talking to me on the phone. I liked him, even if I'd made a mess of things the other night.

"I'll check them out," I told him, not meaning anything much by it.

"You should. I saw a cute little Appaloosa colt there."

I shook my head quickly. As much as I hated to squash whatever little dream he had of me owning a bunch of horses, that was simply not going to happen. "I'm not getting one of them."

He didn't seem fazed by my response. "Sure."

"I'm not."

"Okay."

I pursed my lips at the ceiling. "I can't."

Trent laughed. "I'm not saying anything."

I knew that, but there was also a suggestion in his words, and now I wanted to go check out the Appy colt he'd been talking about. I liked Appaloosas because they were interesting to look at with spots all over them. But that was as far as I went. "Do you want to come over sometime?"

"As friends?"

"Yep." I nodded. There wouldn't be anything more between us.

"Sure. Tonight?"

CAITLIN RICCI

"I'll have a pizza made. Seven?" I asked. It wouldn't be much, since it was just a frozen one, but it was something. And maybe we could go for a walk or something. Or there was always my fairly extensive movie collection. I was pretty proud of it. Having him over for a movie didn't go so well last time, but I thought maybe tonight would be different.

"Sounds good. See you then."

We hung up and I smiled as I got up from the couch and went to the big windows to look out over the pine trees. I knew it wasn't a date since we weren't anything more than friends. But I wished my stomach would realize it and settle down.

SEVEN O'CLOCK came and went, and then at nearly eight, I heard a car coming up my driveway. I was going to be upset at Trent for being so late until I saw his expression through my glass front door and shook my head. He looked like he'd had a rough time of it. I unlocked the door and waited for him to take off his holster and hat, leave them in the car, then come up to my front door.

"I'm sorry I'm late. I had a call," he said as he entered.

"Was it bad?" I asked. I didn't really need to know, since I could tell it hadn't been pleasant just by his face, but I was making conversation as much as anything. I tossed a pizza into the oven, since my first choice of a buffalo chicken pizza was cut up and put into the fridge and I wanted something fresher for my dinner with Trent. I went to my fridge, grabbed him a beer, and poured myself some water. I'd had a beer while waiting for him, and the one I gave him was my last one.

"Thanks," he said as I handed him the beer. "And yeah, it was kind of awful. Domestic violence, which we don't get often here, but this one couple has been a problem for us for a while."

"Were they okay?" I asked as we sat down together at the island. His shoulder nearly touched mine and I tried not to think about it.

56

He turned to give me a look. "You didn't ask if she was okay, just if they were. Thanks for that."

I shrugged. I didn't really know what he was getting at. "Sure."

"You didn't automatically assume it was a man and a woman," he clarified for me.

Frowning, I shrugged. "Why would I? I'm gay. I know there are more relationships than just heterosexual monogamous ones."

He gave me a little smile and took a sip of his beer. "Yeah, I know. But it's refreshing. The guys I work with are very hetero. Most have long marriages and kids my age. It's...." Trent frowned and drank a little more. "Kind of really nice to be around someone who doesn't see the world in a certain way."

"I know what you mean." I put my hands around my water glass and looked down at it. "Trent, I'm sorry about the other night. You wanted to go and I should have let you."

He shook his head and pressed his shoulder, for just the briefest of seconds, against mine. "Don't be sorry. I was having a rough day anyway."

"Do you want to talk about it?" I offered.

"No. Maybe someday. But not right now." He smiled at me, like he was trying to convince me that things were okay with him, that he was okay.

I didn't press him, even though I did see the cracks in his smile and the way his eyes looked sad.

I nodded and tightened my hands on the glass. "Okay. No worries." I licked my lips and thought about if I actually wanted the answer to the next question I was going to ask him. But I really did want to know, despite what knowing could mean. "When you left here, did you find someone else?" I asked bluntly.

He put down his beer and nodded. "Yes."

"Oh." I didn't know what else to say to that.

"I'm not going to apologize for how I am," he told me, sounding defensive as he said it.

I took a long drink of my water before I spoke again. I needed the minute to be able to think. "I didn't expect you to. Or even ask you to. I just wanted to know."

Trent turned to look at me, and there was something in his expression, something about not wanting to be judged, about being angry at me for even asking, about being scared even. I didn't know how to get him to turn that all off and just be with me as my friend. Maybe tonight hadn't been a good idea either.

"Why did you want to know?" he asked.

I didn't have a good answer, or even one really lined up. So I went with the truth as I turned on my stool and looked over at him. "I want you as my friend, and maybe, someday, I might like the chance to see if more could work between us. I think you're hot— you know I do. And I think you want me too. Or at least it seemed like it the other night. I want to know what I'm getting into first, though."

He nodded, and I breathed a little sigh of relief at being able to actually get the words out. "I like you too, Caleb," he told me. "It's been a long time since I've done a relationship though, and I can't do that again right now. I like casual sex because I get my needs met without having to get involved in any other way. I know you can't do that, and that's fine, but if you want to be my friend and actually know about me, then that's where I am."

"I get that," I said gently. He raised his eyebrows as if he didn't believe me, which was a fair assumption considering how little we knew about each other. So I decided to give him some honesty too. "Two months ago I broke things off with someone I'd been with for three years. This person also happened to be my boss, who has been married to his wife for years."

He cringed. "Ouch. Well, then I guess here's to making horrible choices in bed." He raised his bottle of beer and I raised my glass of water. We clinked them together, each of us taking a sip right after, and then I was smiling because yeah, that about summed up what my relationship with Paul had been like.

The pizza was done ten minutes later, and we ate quickly, neither of us saying much, before we walked over to the couch and I chose a movie for us. I didn't think it mattered what we watched since we both kind of seemed lost in our own thoughts, but I chose something upbeat and action-y anyway before I came to sit down next to him. Trent surprised me by putting his arm around my shoulders. We were okay like that, I figured. Friends could do that. Friends could do a whole lot more too, I knew, but I tried not to think about that as we sat together.

"How many guys have you been with?" Trent asked before the movie had even officially started.

"Three," I answered without thinking. Paul, Steven, and Chris. Trent didn't say anything to that so I turned to look at him. "I don't think I want to know your number."

He shrugged. "Maybe. Maybe not. We're not having sex, so it's probably not even an issue worth mentioning. I do actually know it, though. I'm not that weird."

"Then why ask me?"

He didn't have a good answer for that, just pursed his lips as if he was refusing to say anything.

I settled back against his arm and tried not to think about it. But I couldn't help it as I pictured him with some guy on the same night I'd nearly slept with him. "Was he any good?" I asked. I really didn't want to know about it. I didn't want to have any more images in my head of him fucking some other guy.

"Who?"

"The guy you had sex with after I told you no," I said bluntly, because I was a little annoyed at him for not figuring out what I meant.

He gave me a look and shook his head. "You don't want the details."

Well that was true enough, but that didn't mean I didn't want my question answered. I was sure he could figure out a way to give me one without the other. "No, I don't want a play-by-play. But just tell me if he was good."

"Why?" Trent stalled.

Irritated, I blew out my breath. "Because I want to know?"

Trent shrugged, and I did get my answer, though. "He wasn't awful. But he didn't mean anything to me either, so he couldn't have been that good."

It was an answer, of sorts, I supposed. But then again it really wasn't. "How often do you have sex with random guys?" I continued.

Instead of answering me, Trent used his body in a move that was far too fast for me to counter as he pushed me down so I was on my back on the couch and he was over me with his body between my legs. "Umph," I groaned as he pressed into me, putting his weight on my stomach and chest.

"If I hold you down like this, will it keep you from asking more questions?"

It wouldn't. I knew that much. "Why? Don't you want to answer them?"

He frowned and shook his head. With him on top of me like this, I could feel everything about him, including that he was a little hard. I wondered if it was because he was lying on me or if it was because he was thinking about the guys he'd been with recently. "People don't know about the guys I have sex with, Caleb. It's not something I advertise, and it sure as hell isn't something I'm particularly proud of. When I hook up with people, I usually don't know their first names. Then I have sex with them and never talk to them again. Sometimes we don't even do much talking while we're having sex. More often than not they call me random names of guys they'd rather be having sex with anyway, and I think about the people I'd rather be with too. It's not a great, earth-shattering experience. The only reason you know is because I want to be friends with you and real friends are typically honest with each other. So could you please stop with the questions about it?"

I stared at him for a long time and eventually he simply laid his forehead against the side of my neck and went still on top of me. I didn't know what to say or even really where to begin. Everything he was talking about was stuff I couldn't—and wouldn't—do. It sounded dangerous and empty. I'd judged Paul for his number, but I had the feeling Trent's was even higher. The difference, though, and the thing that mattered most to me, was that Trent was willing to be honest with me whereas Paul had never even tried to be.

CHAPTER SIX

Trent

CALEB WAS thankfully silent for a while after I lay down on top of him. It was nice to lie there, to feel someone under me, to feel connected to someone without having to be naked with him. But then he opened his mouth, and I wished I had something to stuff in there to shut him up.

"Where do you even find these guys?" he asked.

I wasn't up for arguing with him or answering any more of his questions so without lifting up my head I took out my phone, swiped my finger across it to unlock it, and then showed him the app I used when I needed to have sex with someone. I used it enough that I knew where it was on my home screen without having to actually look at the phone.

"Hot Guy Hookups?" he read, sounding a bit incredulous as he took my phone from me. I should have pinned his arms down too because he started going through the app without even asking me first. I guess since I'd handed the phone to him that was permission enough, but still, I didn't want him seeing the kind of people I'd had sex with recently, which were all starred automatically from the home page of the app. Their reasoning was that I needed easy access to them in case I wanted to get together with them again. My thinking, though, was that I needed help remembering who I'd already been with on there so I knew to avoid them.

"You had sex with him?"

I lifted my head up to see which profile he'd clicked on. Denver guy, early forties, bald, and with a little bit of a stomach. I'd still found him attractive enough. "Yeah." I put my head back down on his shoulder.

"Him too?"

I didn't want to put my head up again. "What's he like?"

"TieMeUpDaddy69."

I snickered at his username but unfortunately that wasn't enough to go on for me. "Is there a little star next to his name?"

"Yes. That mean something?" Caleb asked.

Nodding, I shifted my weight on him to make it more comfortable for me. If he didn't like the change, he didn't say anything. "Means I met up with them, which typically means I had sex with them. Not always, but generally."

"Ohhh."

"Yep. Now you know all my dirty little secrets." I'd meant it as sort of a half joke, which it really wasn't. I enjoyed sex, but I knew the difference between the stupid sex I had with the people on that app and the actual sex I could have with someone I genuinely liked. One was like exercise; the other I hadn't had in years.

"And you never call any of them back?"

I wasn't sure why it sounded like that was so hard for him to believe. "No. I never do." I lifted my head and pressed my hips a little against him. We were trying to be friends, but it was hard for me to lie there on top of him and feel his cock right beneath mine and not get affected by it. He blushed a little, and I knew he'd felt my movement, as small as it was, too.

"Why not?" he asked. I couldn't believe we were still having this conversation.

"Because they didn't mean anything to me the first time around. Why would that change on the second?"

He shrugged and lifted one of his hands to lay it over my shoulder. I couldn't help noticing how hot he really was. He was tanned, likely from too much time spent in the sun in LA, but he wasn't overly muscular like some of the beach guys I saw on TV. His thighs were what did me in, though, even now as they pressed against my hips. He had muscular thighs, the kind a person didn't get from sitting at a desk all day. I rolled my hips against him, and he bit his bottom lip.

"Trent... I can't."

I might have been mean for doing that to him, especially since I knew he wasn't into casual sex. But the thing was, I didn't want to just fuck him right then, though I would have gladly taken that opportunity. I wasn't needy or on edge, and I didn't feel like my skin was crawling and the only way to get it to stop was to spend all my energy fucking some complete stranger.

No, for once I was completely in the moment with someone, just like I had been years ago. I hadn't felt that kind of draw since Simon, and even though I knew I wouldn't be having sex with Caleb tonight, just rubbing against him was enough for the moment.

"I know you don't want to have sex. I'm not going to get you to change your mind in one night. I know that," I reassured him.

"Then what...?" I rolled my hips again and felt him rise up to meet me this time. He might not have wanted to have sex, but he certainly wasn't immune to me. "What are you doing?"

I shrugged and leaned back down to press my forehead against his neck. I stopped moving on top of him, and he kept one of his hands on my shoulder. It wasn't fair to either of us that I turned us both on when I had no intention of finding someone in Denver to screw and Caleb had no reason to have sex with me.

"Messing around," I confessed against his neck.

"It's not fair."

I smiled. "But it felt good." He had no argument for that. "You okay?" I asked. I wanted to make sure I wasn't crushing him by being comfortable on top of him.

"Aside from being hard and not really having a good way to deal with it? Yeah, I'm perfect."

I laughed. I was in the same boat as him. "Have you ever tried casual sex?" I asked, even though I was pretty sure I knew the answer. Most people who had only ever had three partners in their lives didn't try the no-strings-attached kind of pleasure.

"No. And I'm not interested now."

I shrugged and kissed the side of his neck, because it was right there in front of me and also because I could. He was able to tell me to get off and I would have, so I was comfortable touching and kissing him where I wanted to, within reason of course. We could still be friends who sometimes kissed, I figured. I'd had friends like that in college, though they were more fuck buddies than friends, so maybe that wasn't the best example.

"Never said you had to be. Just asked a question." I reached down to grab on to the bottom of his shirt and felt him jerk against my hand as I rested my fingertips against his belly. "How bad was your accident?" It was a strange question to jump to, but when I'd asked if he was okay, I was mostly trying to figure out if I was hurting his back.

He groaned, and I felt it in my chest, which made me smile. "That's a whole sordid tale on its own."

"I've got time," I promised.

"You don't have to run off to go get someone to take care of you?"

He was joking, kind of, but being a cop meant I was used to hearing the lies in people's words and the little things they didn't want me to hear in their otherwise normal conversations. Caleb may have been trying to joke, but I heard the pain and a bit of jealousy in his voice. I moved my head forward to kiss the big muscle that ran along the side of his neck. "No. I'm good here. It's only on the bad days that I need to find someone or else go insane. You happened to catch me on one of them the other day."

"And you won't tell me what it was?"

I shook my head. I hadn't even told my dad yet about what was happening with Simon next month. "No."

65

"Okay." He took a deep breath. "So the person who hit me with her car was my boss's wife." I groaned, already expecting this story to get a lot worse. "Oh no, it's not over quite yet," he said. I knew it. "She found out about us somehow. I don't really know, but he made himself out to be the victim. So while I was driving the company car to a meeting, she rear-ended me. Then when the police and ambulance were coming, she got out of her car, and screamed at me like a crazy person for seducing her husband and tricking him into having sex with me."

I laughed as I pictured it, but then I remembered he'd gotten hurt and stopped laughing. "Are they still together?"

"Of course."

"Are you jealous?" I asked.

Caleb snorted, and I smiled at his neck, since that's all I could see of him without lifting my head. "No. Not at all. I had thought I loved him, once upon a time, but when it became pretty obvious he was never going to leave her for me, I stopped feeling like that."

I nodded and gave his neck a kiss, which made him squirm. So I tried it again and got the same response.

"Your beard tickles," he said. I could hear the smile in his voice.

I took my hand off his stomach, even though I really didn't want to, and touched the side of my face. "I don't have a beard," I protested.

"Your stubble, then. It tickles."

I rubbed my cheek against his neck just to feel him jump against me again. Him moving around like that was making it hard for me to lie still on top of him, though. I reached down and held on to his hip, forcing him to stop moving as I laid my head against the side of his neck again. "Stop. It's too much."

He must have realized what I meant because he stopped moving on his own and just relaxed. He still felt so good, though, even doing nothing beneath me. He curled his fingers in my shirt over my shoulder, and I forced myself not to rub against him. I

66

wasn't close or anything like that, and I wouldn't be rushing off to find someone to have sex with, but I didn't want to be uncomfortable with a hard cock I couldn't do anything about either. The movie was still playing, but I had no idea what was going on. Maybe we'd watch another. It was still early enough that we could hang out for a few more hours, and I didn't want to be the one to ruin it just because I was hard for him.

"I want you," I said softly against his neck, in case he hadn't noticed that already.

He nodded. "I want you too, Trent. But I can't...."

I wasn't an asshole. I wasn't saying I wanted him to have sex with me right then and there, though if he offered, I wouldn't turn him down. "I know. I just wanted you to know what I'm feeling right now is for you. In case you were wondering."

I shrugged and felt him go even softer under me, like he'd let go of some tension he'd been hanging on to or something. "Thanks. I think I needed to hear that."

Nodding, I released his hip and put my hand back on the small patch of his stomach that I'd exposed. That pinned my hand between us, but it wasn't so bad that I was uncomfortable. "Do you want me to get up?"

"Not necessarily. Are you comfortable?"

"Very. I could go to sleep just like this."

He laughed. "Maybe don't do that. I don't know if I'm strong enough to get you off me."

"You don't need to be stronger. It's all about leverage. You could easily get me off you right now." I'd taught self-defense for a few months before someone older, more experienced, and less attractive had taken over the classes for me. One of the guys on the force had told me it was my lack of experience. My dad told me the truth, though. They were getting e-mails from women asking for my number after having a class with me. That's when I started taking over the e-mails too, so the other guys didn't have to deal with my fan mail, my dad had said. There weren't that many guys on the force, twelve at most usually, and I was the youngest of them all.

"What you would do is wrap your outside leg around one of mine and then twist yourself. That's the easiest way to explain it and—*umph!*" I didn't expect him to do it right then, but suddenly I was on the floor, and he was sprawled out on top of me.

"Is your back okay?" I asked. I hadn't really thought about how twisting like that could hurt him.

But he sat up and rested his hands on my chest for balance. I tried not to think that he was sitting over my lap. "Yeah. Feels okay for right now. I still desperately need to find a chiropractor."

I chuckled and took a chance at putting my hands on his upper thighs. "Good luck there. We don't have any in Thornwood. I know that for sure."

He chuckled, and he probably didn't mean to rub against me just right, but whatever he did sent a wave of pleasure straight through me and had me digging my fingers into his thighs. "Get off me," I groaned as I looked up at him.

"Not as much fun being the one on the bottom, is it?" he teased. And as he pushed against me again, this time curling his fingers into my chest, I realized he was doing it on purpose, which bordered on being cruel since I knew he didn't want to have sex.

I could have easily put him under me again, and I was tempted to, but I didn't want to risk hurting his back. So I lay there and took it as he rubbed against me and left me gritting my teeth because I couldn't do anything else to him besides grab his hips, which I was already doing.

"You're not being fair," I ground out.

"I know. But you weren't either."

Finally he did get off me, and I sat down on the floor next to him with my back against the couch. "Fuck," I snapped out as I rubbed my hand over my swollen cock. "You knew exactly what you were doing to me."

Caleb shrugged, and I let my head fall back against the sofa. "I've had sex before, so yeah, I know how to turn a guy on. You do too, so don't act all innocent with me like you didn't know what you were doing either."

"Sure you don't want to get naked and take care of each other?" I asked, even though I already knew the answer.

But my question took him out of his lighter mood and brought a frown to his face. "I do like you, Trent, but I can't have sex with you after just a week. That's not how I am."

I nodded and struggled up to my feet. "I know. So where's your bathroom?"

"Are you seriously going to come in my bathroom?" Caleb asked, as if he couldn't believe my nerve.

I leveled a glare at him. "Unless you're planning to suck me, then yeah, I do want to get this taken care of. I might have been able to walk around and hang out with you when I was almost hard but not fully. That's not the case anymore, and I'm hurting. So either fix this or tell me where your bathroom is."

He rolled his eyes but lifted his hand anyway. "Little hall by the stairs. Second door on your left. Don't make a mess!" he called after me as I walked away. I waved to him over my shoulder to let him know I'd heard him before I found the bathroom, pulled down my pants, and took my hard cock into my hand. "Fucking Caleb," I groaned as I started stroking myself. His thighs had felt good under my fingertips and having him grip me on my shirt was just what I'd needed too. I guess we'd turned each other on, but I tried to be good because he told me no. He, on the other hand, had intentionally left me frustrated as a way of paying me back, it seemed, for what I'd done to him. And now here I was, in his bathroom, jerking off while thinking about being buried in his ass so deep that I could grip his hips and grind against him as I came inside him.

In my fantasy he panted my name and begged for more. That was the part that did me in, where I pictured his face flushed the way it had been the first time I'd seen him, as he begged me not to stop, to keep going, to come in him.

"*Fuuck*," I growled as large streams of my come shot into his toilet. I was the one left flushed and panting as I cleaned up and put myself away. I ran cold water over my face before coming out to see him again, only to find myself in an empty living room.

I could have hung around and waited for him, and maybe I should have. But instead I went looking for Caleb, and once I found him I was glad I had. He was on his back on a big bed. He hadn't even bothered to fully close the door so I came inside and left it a little open, just as he had. His jeans were pushed down his hips and his shirt was pulled up over his stomach. He didn't have a lot of definition to his abs, but he had enough that I was licking my lips as I waited to taste them.

But as soon as Caleb saw me, he stopped touching his hard cock and quickly tried to cover himself with the dark green sheet near his hip. "Shit," he cursed.

I didn't care that I'd caught him jerking off since I'd just finished downstairs myself. I wished we could have done it together, but whatever. I planned to get another chance to do that. I crossed my hands behind my back and leaned against the wall across from him. Maybe I was trying to show him I wasn't going to touch him or try to convince him to have sex with me. Maybe I was just trying to get comfortable since there was no way in hell I was leaving that room until I got to watch him come.

Either way, I lifted my eyebrows and waited for him to continue.

"You're not leaving, are you?" he asked.

I shook my head. "Why should I?"

He didn't tell me to go, and I didn't leave on my own. Instead he pulled the sheet aside, giving me a good view of his thick cock and swollen head, then stroked himself again. "If I had known you were coming up here, we could have done this together," I said conversationally.

He gave me a look as if he couldn't believe I was still standing there, just watching him. I didn't mind, but it sucked that I couldn't touch him. I could have tried, but I was pretty sure that if I went up to touch him, he would stop what he was doing, fix his clothes, and that would be the end of it. I knew he wasn't into casual sex, and I wasn't getting laid by him tonight, but I still desperately wanted to run my fingers down the little trail of hair that wound over his stomach to end in a blond patch of curls just a few shades darker than the hair on his head.

"I thought about you while I came in your bathroom," I told him, as if it was the most natural thing in the world.

"Oh yeah? What about?" If he was trying to play it off as being cool, he wasn't doing a very good job of it because I could hear the hitch in his breath each time the long strokes of his hand got up to the head of his cock. I preferred shorter strokes. It was surprising, for me at least, that he went from the base of his cock, right on top of his balls, all the way back up to his head each time.

I smiled at him and brought one of my hands from behind my back to rub the front of my pants. I wasn't hard, but I could be soon enough if he would just give in. Since that wasn't going to happen, I touched myself only long enough to see his face flush an even darker shade of red before he lifted his gaze from my crotch back to my face.

"Having you bent over in front of me, my cock buried so deep in your ass that I could grind my hips against you as I dug my fingers into your hips." He wasn't even pretending not to be affected by me anymore as he groaned and rolled his head to the side.

I came away from the wall and went to the foot of his bed. I still didn't touch him, but I was close enough to touch his foot if I thought I could get away with it. Unfortunately his foot was not the part of him I most wanted to touch right then.

"When I made myself come, I thought about coming in you and filling your ass," I continued. My voice dropped on its own without me even trying, and I smiled as I saw his hips buck off the

71

bed. "You wanted me to go harder, faster. And you begged me for more. That's what did me in. I imagined the sound of you begging when I fucked your tight ass as hard as I could."

He groaned and jerked when he came. I stepped forward and ran my hand up the inside of his leg, starting at his ankle and moving up his calf until I cupped his thigh right below his open fly. Caleb was watching me as I bent and slid my mouth over his stiff cock. He hissed out a moan, and I was pretty sure he didn't know what he should do in that moment because I had finished cleaning off his head with long swipes of my tongue before he put his clean hand on my shoulder. He could have pushed my head down; I wouldn't have minded. But it was nice to feel his fingers curl into the material of my uniform, just as they had when we were on the couch.

I took my time cleaning him up because it let me enjoy his taste. I knew what I wanted from him, but there were no guarantees with him. And if this was the only time I would ever get to put my mouth on his cock, I was sure as hell going to enjoy the feeling of having him in my mouth and the taste of his come on my tongue. His heavy panting had turned into soft sighs by the time I was done with him.

I was half-hard again, and if he would have let me fuck him right then, I would have easily been able to get it up the rest of the way. But I could tell from looking at his face that what we'd done was as far as he was going to let things go that night. Which, fine, I could handle that. I didn't want to stop there, but I certainly wasn't going to be an asshole about it either.

"There's a master bath through that door with some mouthwash on the sink if you need it," he said as I straightened back up.

I shook my head. "I don't mind your taste."

He blushed again, though he hadn't actually stopped blushing since I came into his bedroom, and slowly got off the bed. He zipped himself up, then went into the bathroom to clean up the rest of the way. He left the door open so I got to see him take a wet washcloth and run it over his stomach where I hadn't licked him clean.

"I don't know how being friends with you is going to work," he said as he came back out and tossed the washcloth into his hamper.

"Meaning what?" I asked.

Caleb shrugged and stuffed his hands into his pockets. "I've never been friends with someone I wanted to have sex with so much."

There was an easy answer for that, but I figured he probably already knew what I was going to say. And I didn't want to drive him away by repeating myself. "Want to try again tomorrow? One more time? I'll bring over a movie we can actually watch." I was trying to be good, and I hoped he saw that, because the alternative was me having him bent over the dresser he was standing next to and fucking him from behind until he cried out and came all over it.

Caleb gave me a quick nod. "I'd like that. Do you think it could even work, though?"

"I don't know. I'm not really friends with many people," I admitted.

"That you don't have sex with?" he asked.

I laughed and shook my head. "No. In college, yes. But recently not so much. Guys at the precinct, people at the diner that have known me since I was a baby, but not really guys like you. So I'm trying not to fuck this up with you."

Smiling, Caleb came forward and gave me a hug. It was strange hugging a guy I wanted, since I didn't do that with the guys I had sex with, but I had to admit that it felt good to have him in my arms.

"I appreciate you trying," Caleb said.

I nodded. "I know you don't want casual sex."

He stepped away, and I didn't try to stop him. "Yeah, I really can't do that. I know it works for you, and I'm sure it's frustrating, just like it is for me. But I would want to date you, to have a relationship with you. Go to movies and share milkshakes at the diner."

That all sounded nice, but that wasn't something I could give him. Someone could, and I wouldn't try to get in the way of him finding someone else if he wanted to, but I couldn't be that kind of guy for him.

"Tomorrow, then?" I asked. I could tell he was disappointed that I didn't say I could do all of those things with him. I'd be his friend, absolutely, but I couldn't be anything more serious than that with him. And I wasn't ready to tell him why either.

Caleb nodded. "Yeah. See you tomorrow."

I could have stayed around; we might have been able to watch the movie from the beginning. But I could tell he was done for the night, and I was too. A week of knowing Caleb had turned what I wanted in a guy completely around, but I couldn't do anything about that right then.

CHAPTER SEVEN

Caleb

HALFWAY THROUGH a phone meeting with one of my regular clients the next morning, I was distracted enough to visit the Green Acres Equine Sanctuary's website. I instantly knew I needed to update it for them because whoever had designed it had no idea what they were doing. Large portions of the text were unreadable and many of the images had to be scrolled over to be viewed fully, despite how large my monitor was. I shook my head and went through their recent rescue pictures, looking for any good ones of Trent.

"What's that color between purple and blue that I like?" Mr. Riti asked.

"Violet?" I answered blandly. He wanted a family website with each of his twelve grandchildren getting their own page with their own color scheme. It was good money, but I was pretty sure the finished product would look awful. "Are you sure you don't want to go with one color scheme for the site as a whole? It would make it look more uniform."

"My grandchildren aren't uniform!" He sounded as if I'd somehow offended him. I filed that away as something to remember when working with him again, because he always wanted something new every few months it seemed.

"Of course not. Violet for your oldest, then?" I said in an effort to calm him down. I had a good reputation and enough clients and repeat work that I could afford to say no to some of them, especially the ones with a bad history of not paying me on time, but Mr. Riti wasn't like that. He was a bit extreme sometimes, but he paid me on time and always came back for more work. Two of his kids had even requested work from me too.

"Yes, violet for her. And then royal blue for the next one. That's a pretty color, isn't it?" he asked.

"It is." I still didn't know if he wanted the text, the background, or some heading to be these colors but that was something I'd figure out when I actually got started on his project and got more of the specifics from him. This was just the talking stage, which really could have been done by e-mail and would have let me search for pictures of Trent a lot more easily. But Mr. Riti was one of my clients who actually liked to talk things through, no matter how little I did. He'd booked me for an hour, though, and was paying me for my time as well, so I saved one quick picture of an exhausted-looking, very dirty, Trent where he was smiling as he closed up a horse trailer before I clicked out of the website and focused completely on Mr. Riti and his latest website project.

The entire project, including calendars he decided to spring on me just as I was about to hang up the phone, would take me a couple of weeks to manage. The great thing about working from home was that I didn't have to waste an hour each way driving in traffic to get to an office to do things I could have just as easily done at home, and done them better and faster there too. The office in LA had always been distracting to me with people talking nonstop and doors closing excessively hard since they were the heavy kind that no one really used anymore. Except for Paul.

Great. That was one person I hadn't meant to think about. He'd been respecting my space, for the most part, which was nice. But I was still getting random naked texts. I deleted them instantly, but I wasn't sure how to make it any clearer that I did not want to have anything more to do with him. He was a liar and he slept around. I felt guilty for thinking that, though, since Trent slept with a lot of guys too, but at least he didn't lie to me about it. In fact, I was sure that if I actually texted him and wanted to know if he'd been with anyone in the last few days, he would tell me. And I was also pretty sure I would know the answer to that question already without even having to ask. I shouldn't have been comparing them at all, except I didn't have a lot else to go on between them. I'd thought I loved Paul. Wasn't it natural to want to examine my ex against the feelings I was starting to have for someone else?

I sighed and ran my hands through my hair in frustration. I wanted him, but I couldn't be something on the side. Not again. The worst part of it was that I kept getting the feeling that he was holding back from me, that sex was all Trent could give me. I wanted him so much and sometimes I thought I could handle that. People had sex with their friends all the time; there were even really bad movies about it. But I wasn't like that. I'd been with three guys, and even though I hadn't had sex with him, I counted Trent in that number now, which brought me up to a whole four people, just because he'd put his mouth on my cock.

I was starting to get hard just thinking about him slowly cleaning me off. He didn't suck me, didn't even put much pressure on me, but that had been more than enough to last me for a few fantasies.

Going back to the horse sanctuary page to keep looking for more pictures of him was an easy decision. I had work I could have been doing, and even if I didn't, there was always laundry to do or I could have decided to eat something more than cookies, chips, and the remainder of the beef jerky I'd brought over from California. I had some boxed macaroni and cheese I could have made for lunch, since it was nearly eleven, but I was a bit too lazy for that, and besides, there were pictures of Trent in front of me.

He looked happy with the horses, and I kind of wished I could get one to see him that happy in person. Which was a horrible idea and would never actually happen, but I was going through their fostering requirements anyway. I didn't want to adopt a horse, since I couldn't guarantee I'd be able to take care of it if something happened to me, but if I could foster one while Dean, Natalie, and Sam were visiting, then that could be good for the kid. As far as I knew, Sam had never really been around horses. I didn't count pony rides at carnivals as actually riding, so I was pretty sure he hadn't. There wasn't much to it though, I remembered, aside from vet visits, farriers, tack, feed, and everything else that added up to a very expensive pet.

But according to the website, they covered all that. Before I could change my mind, I filled out the foster volunteer form on their website. If they weren't coming out, then I wouldn't foster, but I was pretty sure Natalie was ready to get her kid out of LA for a while. It made me really mad that some kids hurt him for being gay, and I was proud of him for coming out and being that brave. I hadn't been at his age, but Sam had always been the kind of kid who was pretty sure of who he was and what he wanted. I admired that about him.

It was nearly noon when I looked away from my laptop again and cheap pasta and fake cheese didn't really sound all that appealing. Normally I loved macaroni and cheese, but the boxed stuff just wasn't going to do it for me right then. I got off the stool, rubbed my sore back—I'd spent far too much time leaning over the island—then left the house to go to Rosie's for lunch. I figured I'd stop by the store and get some more essentials afterward, and maybe I'd even see Trent there with the other cops.

I was right. He was there, and he was surrounded by other people. Still, when I came in, he raised his hand and waved to me. I waved back, shot him a smile, and then followed a waitress over to a booth. Pulled pork, sweet potato fries, and sweet tea sounded like a good lunch, though not particularly healthy. It was a good thing I wasn't trying to be healthy, then, I supposed....

Halfway through my lunch, Trent pulled himself away from the guys at his table to come join me. He stole two of my fries, which I guessed was fair since I remembered taking a few of his before, but when he reached for my pulled pork I nearly stabbed him with my fork in defense of my lunch.

Laughing, he shook his head, then finished up with a grin at me. I was the center of his attention for that moment, and it was nice to have all of him focused solely on me. "How's work going?" I asked.

Trent shrugged and rested his arms on the table. "Decent, I guess. I spent most of the morning answering e-mails so I can't complain. How's designing going? Anything fun?"

I thought over my morning and how I'd applied to be a foster, but I didn't want to tell him that in case I was rejected. I thought he would have been really excited, and I didn't want him to get his hopes up. Maybe, if I did get to foster a horse though, he could take care of it too. As if he needed another reason to be over at my house most nights. "Nothing too major," I finally said. "Grandfather wanting to make a website for his family. Easy stuff."

"Have you ever designed anything really fun?" He leaned toward me, and I figured I knew exactly what he was asking. Fortunately I did have a story for him.

"Well… there was this one college-boy porn site once…," I quietly told him with a wink.

He groaned and we shared grins. "We still on for tonight?" he asked.

I nodded. "A movie sounds good." I had the suspicion that I should have clarified that porn wasn't a movie, especially after revealing I'd built a porn site for a client once, but I didn't think that was really necessary. At least I was pretty sure I didn't have to tell him that.

I wanted to ask him if he'd be going out after, if he had a date with one of his nameless guys after our movie, but I couldn't bring myself to. I didn't want to know about that and I didn't want to embarrass him in the middle of his mom's diner. It was enough that I knew he had guys lined up and waiting for him, and that if I wanted to be, I could have easily been counted in that number. But that's all it would have been. Friends who had sex, friends who screwed around, watched movies, drank beer, shared fries at a diner, but nothing more.

It was tempting. Oh God, it was so tempting to just accept that kind of friendship from him when he was that close to me and wearing that ridiculously unflattering police uniform that he still managed to somehow make look really good. But I had to have a bit more self-control, and I needed more from him. The sex would be great, I was sure of it, but I couldn't pretend it would be anything more than that. Not when he wasn't willing to commit to me. And really, I reminded myself, we'd known each other for a little over a week. Asking anyone to commit after such a short time was insanity.

"You okay? You look kind of upset," Trent said as he reached out and briefly brushed his hand over mine.

I nodded and tried to put on a happy face. It didn't work so well. "Yeah. I'm good. I was just thinking."

He gave me a little smile and I smiled back. "You're not reconsidering getting together tonight are you?"

"Of course not."

"Good. Didn't want whatever was upsetting you to get in the way of the fantastic action-slash-horror movie I plan to bring over tonight."

I groaned just at the sound of the combination. "Great. Two of my favorite genres put together. If the movie is awful, though, you have to bring beer the next time you come over."

"And if it's not and you end up loving it, then I get a kiss," Trent countered with a pretty evil grin.

I glanced around the diner to see if anyone had heard, but no one was paying attention to us. Well, not no one precisely. There was one older gentleman in a suit who had been sitting with Trent and who was now openly watching me as if I were a teenager at some expensive clothing store and he was worried I was going to shoplift.

"Who's the guy with the grayish hair in the suit over there?" I asked as I finished off my pulled pork. He'd taken most of my fries, so I ended up pushing the rest toward him anyway.

Trent glanced over at the table and nodded to the man I'd asked about. "Him? That's my dad. Can I have some of your tea?"

"No. Get your own. And your dad?" I looked over at him again and lifted my hand to give him a wave. He waved back to me, and I turned around to face Trent, who was drinking my tea. I rolled my eyes and chose to ignore that part. I had more important things to focus on. "Do you want me to meet him?" I asked.

Trent finished drinking my tea, thankfully leaving me a little, then shrugged. "Sure. I mean, if you want to. Everyone in town knows him, so you might as well."

The way he'd said it reminded me that we weren't together; we were just friends. He'd seen me practically naked, and I'd had my hand around his cock, but we weren't anything serious, and if I wanted to meet his dad, I could. I got up from the booth and walked over to introduce myself to the father of the man I wanted, the man I was starting to care about, but someone I could only know as a friend.

"Hey, I'm Caleb Robinson. I'm friends with Trent, and I moved into the big cabin on the hill down the road," I said as I stuck out my hand.

He gave me an assessing once-over before hitting me with a big smile that told me just where Trent got his. "Good to have you in Thornwood," he told me as he got up from the table and shook my hand. "Come over sometime. I'll make burgers," he tacked on.

"Thanks." I dropped his hand as Trent came up behind me.

"We gotta go," he said. There were groans around the table, and I stepped back to give them all space in the crowded diner. I went back to my table, ordered a slice of apple pie, and watched Trent get his keys and wallet together while I waited for it to come.

He was ridiculously good-looking, and if I just gave in, I could have him whenever I wanted. The temptation to do just that was never greater than when he smiled. He was talking to the guys as he walked past me and out of the diner, so I wasn't surprised that he didn't say bye. But he did squeeze my shoulder as he walked by, and I reached up to briefly touch his hand.

Dean called me as I was leaving the diner and getting back into my SUV. "Hey," I said, answering the call.

"Hey. Is it still okay if we come out to visit?"

He sounded uncertain like maybe my invitation had had some sort of time restriction on it. "Of course it is. You all can come out whenever. Or just send Sam out to me if you can't get away. It's a tiny town, and there isn't too much he could actually get in trouble with here." He could have gotten lost in all the government land that ran behind my house, but I didn't say that to Dean. He didn't need another reason to worry about his kid.

"Two weeks from today okay?"

I was already in the grocery store's parking lot. "Yep. Want me to pick you up at the Denver airport?"

"Is it really far?"

I shrugged. "Not really. Let me know all the details, and I'll come get you. If you want, I could cover the plane fare too." He hesitated, and it was like I could hear the dilemma play out in his mind. I had plenty of money I wasn't using. We'd been friends for years and his refusal of my help drove me absolutely nuts sometimes. I could help and I didn't mind doing so, but I did get being proud and stubborn too, and Dean was both of those things.

"Sure. I mean, if it's not a big deal to you."

I was practically stunned that he'd actually allow me to do that for him and his family. I tried to play it cool, though. "It's okay. Totally fine." I rolled my eyes at myself. I wasn't good at playing things off at all.

Dean chuckled, and I was sure he knew what I'd been trying to do. At least he didn't call me out on it, though. "See you in two weeks, then."

"For sure."

We hung up, and I opened my browser to the furniture store's web page. I'd need a few more things before they arrived because my friend and his wife were not sleeping on my sofa bed for however long they wanted to stay with me. I hoped it was for a while. That might make things with Trent a little difficult to juggle, but I really needed to have my friends around me again.

Grocery shopping was easy, since it was just me and the biggest thing I needed was beer, but I tried to go for healthier options this time too. Like Greek yogurt and microwave popcorn. I was pretty sure that still counted as healthy, despite the woman at the register giving me a strange look as I checked out in her line. Maybe it was the handful of candy bars I'd added to my order at the last minute that did it.

Either way, it didn't really matter. I had my groceries and when I got home there was someone in my driveway waiting for me. I got out of my SUV with my bags and went around the back of my vehicle to see a guy at least five years younger than myself holding a clipboard and jotting things down with a pen.

"Hi. Can I help you?" I asked.

He tucked his pen behind his ear and held the clipboard close to his chest so I couldn't see anything he'd been writing. "Are you Caleb Robinson?" he asked.

I frowned since I had no idea what this was about, but I didn't really like coming home to random people in my driveway. I moved from LA to get away from so many weirdos, not that this guy was one of them, but it was still odd to find someone waiting for me to get home. "Yes. You're on private property. You know that, don't you?"

He pushed his glasses up farther on his nose and pulled a business card out of his pocket. "I'm Eli, from Green Acres."

"I wasn't expecting anyone," I said as I read over his card before letting it fall into one of the grocery bags in my hands. "I didn't even get a response to my application yet."

Eli nodded and looked at me briefly before going back to the clipboard in his hand. "We do surprise assessments. That way people don't have time to put temporary fixes on things then keep the horses in unsafe conditions later on. I need to go through your property and see if you meet our requirements, which, I can tell you, are quite stringent. Very few people pass our inspections."

He was a prissy little thing with his all-important clipboard and thick, dark-rimmed glasses, but I figured I'd have to go through some hoops to foster a horse. The experience was making me glad I'd never wanted to foster children, though, if people like Eli were who I had to look forward to on that front. "Well, I need to get these groceries inside and put away. I'll be in the house when you're done." I could have left it at that, but I was feeling a bit put off. "Also, this holier-than-thou thing you've got going on is a bit of a turnoff. I didn't put in a foster application to be treated like I'm going to abuse whatever horse you might potentially send my way. I know you have horses that need homes, and I'm not looking to steal one of them or anything sinister like that."

He stared at me as I turned and went up to the house. I was half tempted to withdraw my application entirely, since I really didn't like Eli or people like him. But then I thought about how happy Trent looked in the pictures, and with a sigh I decided to leave it there. I probably wouldn't get approved anyway.

I had my groceries put away and was about to start drinking my beer when the doorbell rang. I decided Eli could wait a minute and popped open my beer before going to answer the door. "So, what's your verdict?" I asked as I leaned against the doorframe.

"May I come in?"

He sounded a little less like the almighty horse dictator now, so I shrugged and turned around, letting him come in. He closed the door behind himself and we sat down at the island together. "Some of your fences could use a bit of mending or reinforcement," Eli began as he showed me the clipboard. I found myself looking down at a perfectly drawn and exactly to scale map of my barn, pastures, and shelters.

"Did you do this?" I asked.

"Yes. I've marked the spots that have to be seen to in red. You'll need to have those addressed." He tapped the map in case I missed the giant red-marker circles that dotted the back pasture. There hadn't been any attention to the pastures in months, so I wasn't surprised some of them needed work.

"Are you an architect?" I was still surprised at the level of detail he'd managed to get into what was likely a fast drawing.

"No. Now, there is nothing wrong with your barn. I would like your driveway to be paved—"

"So would I, but I'm not doing that yet," I said, cutting him off.

"It makes going up and down the driveway easier on the horses so that they don't go lame after stepping in a rut left by our heavy snow run offs," he continued, as if I hadn't spoken.

I shrugged him off and took a sip of my beer. "You want one?" I offered, remembering my manners now that he wasn't quite so annoying.

Eli shook his head at me. "I'm working."

"I'm not."

He smiled for the first time since I'd met him and pulled the map off the clipboard so I could see another sheet, this one with dozens of questions on it.

"What is your current occupation?" he asked as he pulled the clipboard toward himself and took a bright purple pen from his pocket.

"Graphic designer. I work from home. I make plenty of money, which will not be detailed on your sheet, if that was one of the questions."

He seemed undeterred by my sour reply. "And is your income consistent?"

Some months were better than others, but for the most part things were fine, and I had the settlement to fall back on if I needed to. So I said, "Yes."

"How consistent?" he pestered me.

I rolled my eyes and sipped my beer instead of answering him. But he didn't continue with his interrogation, so I turned to him and waited for him to ask his next question, hoping that I was making it perfectly clear that my finances were fine and also none of his business.

"Fine. I will write down that the applicant refuses to answer the question."

"Damn straight," I told him.

"How long have you been riding?" he continued on. "When you applied, you gave an answer about your experience riding and caring for horses, so I won't be asking you that."

It took me a few minutes to count back that far. "I started when I was six with our neighbor in Kentucky…. Then he moved when I was…." I frowned, not having a good answer. "It's been ten years since I've been on a horse, either way. I'm competent but I'm not going to be training any young horses for your rescue if that's what you think."

Eli kept writing, and I wondered how much longer this was going to take. It was still midafternoon, so I had some time before Trent came over. But I could have probably used a shave. At least the beers would be cold for us to share while watching whatever horrible movie he thought I was going to enjoy. Not likely.

CHAPTER EIGHT

Trent

I PULLED up to Caleb's house a little earlier than I usually did and frowned a bit at the unexpected car in his driveway. He knew I was coming over, so I wasn't sure why there was someone else with him, but I figured it was probably just a client. I was out of my uniform, in a pair of khaki shorts and an old, faded T-shirt, and ready to watch the movie I'd brought with me. He was going to love it, I was sure, which would mean I'd be getting my kiss.

I rang the doorbell and heard Caleb talking to someone before he came to answer it. I saw the surprise on his face when he opened the door and wondered what I'd been interrupting. But then I saw a guy at the island and knew for sure it was just a client meeting by how stiff and proper the other guy looked as he wrote on a clipboard, and I had no reason to be jealous.

"Hey," I said as I came in past him.

"Hi. You're early."

I raised my eyebrows at him and tramped down hard on the bit of jealousy that flared up at his words because that was a sure sign I was interrupting something he didn't want me to know about. But he looked to his big clock on the wall and sighed. "No, actually, you're not really early. This is just taking a lot longer than I thought it would have. Eli, how much longer are you going to keep interrogating me?"

The guy at the island turned around, and I froze as I tried to quickly think of what I was supposed to do in this situation, which had never come up before. This Eli guy, as Caleb seemed to know him, to me was SpankMeHarder5280. He seemed to recognize me too because whatever he was going to say ended up just being a squeak.

"You never texted me back!" He hurled something at me, which ended up being a clipboard with a bunch of papers on it. I read quickly, saw that he was from the rescue I'd just helped, and wondered what the hell Caleb was doing with him.

Instead of answering Eli, because he wasn't important to me, and yes, I had texted him back, once, but I'd stopped responding after his eighth text in a single night, I turned to Caleb. Who, unfortunately, was staring back and forth between us both.

"Caleb—"

"Did you have sex with him?" He cut right to what I was getting ready to explain. It was going to be good and believable and... completely useless now that Caleb had decided to be extremely blunt about things.

"Yes." That was the truth. I'd had sex with him. Once. We met at a gas station, I followed him to a hotel, we had sex, and I left. I didn't even know his name, or actually care about it. "What's he doing here?" I asked, because that was the important piece. Well, one of them, but once I figured out what Eli was doing in Caleb's house, I could find a way to get rid of him so I could actually talk to Caleb, if that's what he needed from me. I wasn't sure if he wanted to talk or if he just wanted to hit me. It could have very easily been both at that point.

"*He* was doing an assessment for a foster volunteer position," Eli snarked at me. I heard him get off the stool and start walking toward me, but all of my attention was focused on Caleb. "And *he* is leaving. Mr. Robinson, I regret to inform you that you did not pass Green Acres' foster application process. Good-bye."

This time I did turn my attention from Caleb to Eli. "On what grounds?" I demanded, because I knew Rocky Creek Stables was excellently kept and gorgeous, or at least it had been when I'd worked there. Any horse would be happy living there, and if Eli was going to be a jackass about it just because I hadn't responded to him when he'd gone all obsessively crazy on me, that was his problem, and he needed to leave Caleb out of it.

Eli looked a little stunned that I'd actually bothered to talk to him. "Caleb hangs out with people I don't want our horses around. Namely you."

Snorting, I shook my head at his audacity. "It was sex. You didn't bother to ask my name; I didn't know yours either. You enjoyed it, so really, what is your problem?" I snapped. Out of the corner of my eye I saw Caleb move to the couch, and I needed Eli gone so I could deal with him, but I wasn't going to let this little shit decide what Caleb could or could not do either.

Eli looked hurt by what I'd said, but I didn't have the slightest idea why. "Mr. Robinson, your application has been approved. Please expect a call this week regarding potential horses that are available for foster care that meet your requirements."

Eli didn't say anything else to me as he walked out the front door. I locked it after him, then came to sit next to Caleb. I didn't know what to say to him and for a while we just sat there in silence.

It was Caleb who broke us out of that uncomfortable moment, though, by saying, "Was he that obnoxious in bed?"

I laughed and took a chance at putting my arm around Caleb's shoulders. He didn't pull away. "Yeah, he kind of was. Caleb, I'm sorry you met one of the guys I've had sex with. I know the casual sex thing is an issue for you, and I never expected you to meet one of them. I drove down to Castle Rock for him, which is over an hour away in case you were wondering. I never thought I'd see him in Thornwood."

Caleb sighed and laid his head back against my arm. "Was it recent?"

"Define recent," I said.

He turned his head to look at me. "Since I've moved here? Since we kissed… since we…?" He swallowed heavily and looked away from me again.

I shook my head. "No. It's been over six months since I saw him."

"I guess that should make me feel a little better," Caleb said, and I winced, knowing he was hurting but not knowing how to make him happy again.

Especially not when I needed to tell him something. "Not that you need any more to think about, but I do want to talk to you about something," I said. I turned toward him on the couch, and he looked over at me again. "And it's not going to be good. But I want you to know."

His expression told me he didn't think it could get any worse. But it could and I knew that. Part of me didn't want to tell him anything at all and let Simon's passing go by with only my dad knowing why I was going to be so upset. But I was trying to be honest with Caleb, and that meant telling him about the bad things that were happening in my life and not just that I was having sex with people he should have never been able to meet.

"Two days from now I need to go down to Denver. I'll probably be out for a few days. I'll have my phone, but I didn't want you to worry in case I didn't pick up right away or return your text or something," I began.

He pursed his lips and closed his eyes for a few moments before opening them again. "Because you'll be there having sex with someone?"

I was quick to shake my head. I reached for his hand, but he didn't let me take it, instead pulling away from me before I could touch him. "No." I took a deep breath and let it out on a sigh. "Five years ago I was in love with someone. His name was Simon, and I honestly thought I'd be spending the rest of my life with him." That got Caleb's attention in a hurry.

"About eight months into our relationship, we were skiing in the mountains here and he lost control. He fell and injured himself pretty badly. He was lucky to survive, but he never woke up again." I found it hard to talk about Simon and very few people knew what had happened. Those people in town who did know we'd been together assumed we'd broken up. I hadn't corrected them.

I licked my lips and kept going with Caleb watching me. "On Thursday his family will be taking him off life support. He's at a hospital in Denver. I'll be going down there to say good-bye. I just...." I didn't know what to say since Caleb had barely moved while I'd been talking. "I just wanted you to know that if I'm not around, if I'm not answering calls, it's because I'm there."

I waited for him to say something, anything, to me. I needed comforting, but I could see he was having a hard time too right now. I tried to touch him again, but he didn't let me. I probably should have waited until after the movie to talk to him about it, but seeing Eli there had made me realize how much Caleb needed to know my biggest secret, since the little ones had hurt him so much already. And I didn't want him hearing it from my dad in case he tried to ask him where I was or something.

"Caleb...." I tried to say something, but I didn't even know where to begin. I just wanted him to speak, to say anything to me. I needed that from him, needed to know that he was okay, that I hadn't lost my only real friend so soon after meeting him.

"I'd like you to go now."

I frowned at him. "What?"

He didn't turn to look at me. "Please get out of my house."

"Don't be like this," I told him as I shook my head. "C'mon, let's talk."

This time he did look at me, and I saw that there were tears in his eyes. "You're in love with someone else. There's nothing for us to talk about. Now please leave. Don't make me call the cops."

"I am the cops," I reminded him. But I did get up and walk toward the front door. "Bye...," I said as I opened the door. He didn't say anything back to me.

I was upset as I left his house, and I did consider going onto the app and finding someone to fix me. But in the end it was easier just to go home, crash out on my bed, and stare up at my ceiling.

I DIDN'T hear from Caleb again until the next afternoon. "Hello?" I answered my phone when I saw it was him calling. I'd been avoiding all other calls but my dad's.

"Do you still love him?" he asked without saying hi.

I was in my apartment even though it was only two in the afternoon. My dad had sent me home early since I was snapping at people over e-mail, even the nice older ladies who wanted to have a handsome police officer at their book club meeting while they talked about some murder mystery. I was off work until the following Monday, which would have been nice except I didn't want to spend my time off with anyone other than the one person who had kicked me out of his house.

"No," I answered honestly. I sat down on my bed and looked out the window at the grocery store. "I did, when he was my Simon. But the man I loved, the one I wanted to be with forever, he's been gone a long time."

"Is he the reason you don't have relationships?" Caleb continued.

"He's the reason I don't want to fall in love again and get hurt," I clarified. I'd loved Simon with everything I had. There was no going back from that kind of love, and I knew sex with strangers wasn't something that was necessarily healthy or good for me. But I was an adult, and I had needs they helped fulfill. There was nothing wrong with what I did, though I was pretty sure Caleb didn't agree with me.

After a few moments of silence during which I let him think, and I stared at a woman trying to juggle a shopping basket and three kids, not a single one of which was behaving as the shopping cart started to roll away from her, he asked, "Do you want a friend to go with you tomorrow?"

"I'd like that. Know of anyone who's available?" I tried to joke with him.

I heard him chuckle, and it made me smile. "What time should I be ready to go?"

"Four probably. It'll take a little while to get down there and find parking. And, Caleb, I got a hotel room for the night since I didn't know if I could handle driving back. I'll reserve one for you too."

I didn't expect him to stay with me in the same room, and I hadn't even considered that as a possibility.

"Reserve it and I'll pay for it myself."

It wasn't right of him for pay for a hotel room because I wouldn't be able to come back up to Thornwood immediately after saying good-bye to Simon, and I was ready to argue with him, but he was apparently done talking to me before I could even begin to say what I wanted to.

"I'll see you tomorrow."

He hung up on me and I sighed as I let the phone fall back onto the bed. I was bored in my townhouse that evening, but I didn't want to go out and see people either. I wanted to go spend time with Caleb, but I knew I probably wouldn't be welcome there, so I watched TV until I started to get drowsy. Eventually I fell asleep on my couch and woke up the next morning feeling exhausted and cranky. To add to it my whole arm was asleep and my fingers hurt to move.

"Fucking perfect," I grumbled as I got started with my day.

My dad called at ten while I was cleaning up my kitchen. Being bored and not knowing what else to do sometimes led me to cleaning. It wasn't something I enjoyed doing, but it had to get done so I did my best to stay on top of it and not get distracted by all the thoughts currently swirling through my head.

"Hey. You doing okay?" he asked as I put him on speakerphone. "It's going to be a tough day for you."

I knew it was and didn't love the reminder, but I did love my dad for calling to check up on me. "I know."

"You need a ride? I can take you if you want."

I shook my head and kept cleaning the sink. "Caleb and I are going down in a few hours. We'll be there overnight and be back tomorrow morning. Just as friends," I tacked on in case he got any ideas.

"I didn't think anything else. Though I do like Caleb, from what little I've seen of him. He has a clean arrest record and only a few parking and speeding tickets from California too. But he needs to get those tags updated."

I groaned and put the sponge down so I could wash my hands. Of course my dad had checked him out.

"I loved Simon too, you know. He was a good guy."

I appreciated that my dad talked about Simon like he was already gone, because to me he was, and it was something I'd asked him to do a few years back when I'd been really ready to let him go. At the hospital, saying good-bye to Simon's body? That was just a formality. My Simon had been gone for years.

"Yeah, he was," I agreed as I dried my hands on a dish towel.

"Don't let what you had with Simon get in the way of what you could have with Caleb," my dad told me in his sternest voice.

I stopped and stared at my phone for a moment. "We're just friends," I reminded him.

"Yes, and you look at every single one of your friends that way. Don't lie to me, boy. Lie to yourself all you want, but not to me. I know that look. Your mom used to look at me the same way. Like she could stay with me forever, like I made everything better. Doesn't matter that Caleb is a man. It's the same look. You care about him."

"It's been two weeks," I told him as I rolled my eyes.

"Your mother was pregnant with you within four days of us knowing each other."

I'd heard that before, but it still made me groan. "I don't need to know that, Dad. Really, I don't. That's not something people tell their kids."

"When their kids are being stubborn, absolutely it is. My point, Trent, is that you don't have to worry about anything here. Let it flow naturally. Don't get held up on time and how long it's been or hasn't been. If you like him, then you like him. I don't want you to stay in love with Simon forever, not when he's not here to love you back."

My dad was right, and he was smart, but he didn't have any idea what he was talking about. Not really, anyway. "I'm not still in love with Simon," I reminded him. I just didn't want to lose another love of my life. One was too much for one lifetime.

At four o'clock I was parked in front of Caleb's house, but I couldn't make myself get out of the car because when I did, well, that would be one more step toward seeing Simon. As much as I'd already said bye to him, as much as I'd given up on ever seeing him awake again, I didn't want to see him officially gone. I thought it was just going to be a formality, but I sat there knowing that if I went to get Caleb, and if we went down to Denver, after his family took him off life support, there would be nothing left of him at all, anywhere.

I realized I was crying only because I suddenly couldn't see. I ran my hands over my eyes and sighed loudly. I had to do this, because if I didn't go see Simon, then this was going to happen without me anyway. And I didn't think I would ever forgive myself for not being there with him one last time.

Forcing myself to get out of my car was the first part. Going up to Caleb's house came next. It didn't become easier with each step I took, like I hoped it would. Instead I stood there just staring at Caleb's door wondering what I should have done differently. Simon loved to ski, loved to be outside, and had climbed more mountains and been scuba diving in deeper caves than I had even before meeting him. He was wild and invincible. He didn't need my influence to get him there. But his sister, Cassandra, likely still thought I'd been the reason for his accident.

With a shaking hand I knocked on Caleb's door. He opened it a few moments later, gave me a once-over, and then backed up.

"We need to get going," I told him weakly, even as I followed him inside the house.

He shook his head and opened one of the cabinets under the island. "This will only take a minute, and you look like you need this." He put a bottle of bourbon on the island then poured a little into a glass. Before he handed it over to me he poured a little water into it from the sink.

"Try it," he said.

I looked down at the amber-colored liquid and hesitated. "I don't normally drink bourbon, or whiskey, or whatever it is." I looked back up at him and tried for a smile, but it didn't really work out that well.

He shook his head and pushed the glass toward me with one finger. It sloshed a little up the sides, and I watched its movement for a moment, letting myself get lost in the ripples before I was pulled out of it by Caleb as he moved around the island toward me. We may have been friends, and I thought we were, but as he walked around me, it was like he was trying his absolute best not to come close enough to touch me. Regardless of the sex, of how much I wanted him, of how hot it had been to have him under me as I ground my hips against him knowing he could feel every single movement... aside from all of that, I wanted my friend to give me a hug right then because I desperately needed one.

I didn't feel right asking him for one, though, so instead I took the glass between my fingers and tilted it against my lips. The bourbon burned, like it always did, and I was instantly reminded of why I didn't usually drink anything heavier than beer.

I gasped as I put the glass down, then managed to get it into the sink, mercifully without coughing enough to show Caleb just how inept I was with the heavy stuff.

"Better?" Caleb asked.

I shrugged and leaned forward over the island.

"Do you usually drink bourbon?" When I'd seen him drink, it had only ever been with beer. Not many people I knew drank bourbon, and I didn't even think the grocery store carried the brand he'd pulled out.

"I'm from Kentucky. We have thoroughbreds and bourbon, among other things, but that's what I really remember from living there. This stuff I had to drive into downtown Denver to get. I figured you might need some for today."

I tried for another smile and actually managed it this time. "You figured right." My smile quickly fled, and I was back to wallowing somewhere between wanting to go back to bed and knowing I needed to go to downtown Denver. "Did you get it last night after we talked?"

He shook his head. "This morning, actually."

"You didn't have to do that. Just for me...." I frowned. It was a bit of a drive to go downtown, especially for a bottle of alcohol. And here I was asking him to drive down with me again so soon. Most people in town hardly ever went into Denver. There were closer places to get the things they needed, or people made do without.

Caleb smiled at me, just a little. "I didn't do it just for you."

"You didn't?" I had a hard time believing that.

With a sigh Caleb shook his head. "I like you, a lot, even though it's only been a few weeks since we met. And you are in love with someone else...." I was about to tell him that he was wrong, that I didn't still love Simon, but I couldn't make myself say the words. So I said nothing and let him believe what he wanted to for the time being. I wasn't up for arguing with him right then. "I wanted to have it handy, in case I wanted some." He shrugged and started heading toward the door. "We should go."

"Caleb...."

At the front door he turned around and held his hands up to me. "Just... don't. Not right now, Trent. I want to be friends, and that means at this moment I'm going to drive us into Denver, and I'm going to be there for you when you need me today. But I'm hurt, and what you did, how you didn't tell me about him, that wasn't okay. So let's get going."

I nodded and followed him out of the house. "I can drive."

Caleb shook his head. "I'm driving. You get to relax and direct me to wherever it is we're going."

I was thankful, and relieved, that I didn't have to focus any more than that. It wasn't that the bourbon was getting to me, though that may have been part of it. I felt a little better, though, with the decision of going being taken away from me.

"I don't still love him," I told Caleb again as we headed out onto the main road.

Caleb didn't say anything, and I turned my head to look out the window instead of arguing with him about something I wasn't absolutely sure of yet myself.

It didn't take us long to get into Denver, only about an hour and a half with traffic, which was pretty decent for the afternoon. Going back tomorrow morning would be faster I was sure. "Take I-25 south for two more exits, then a left, and three blocks up, the entrance to the hospital will be on your right," I told him. I wasn't great at directions, especially to a place I hadn't been to in a long time, but the place where Simon lay alive but not really was a place I couldn't easily forget either.

Instead of dropping me off in front, like I expected him to do, Caleb parked across from the entrance. "Do you want me to come in with you?" he asked as he turned off his SUV.

I didn't answer him at first while I thought things over. I could use him there, since I didn't know how I'd really be able to manage what I knew was coming, but at the same time this was something I had to do, and I didn't know if it was fair that Caleb had to be there with me.

"Do you want to?" I finally just ended up asking him, because I still hadn't decided what the right answer was.

Caleb shrugged and leaned a bit over the steering wheel as he looked up at the tall tan-colored hospital. "I want to be there for you. You're my friend."

I didn't like that word coming from him so much, because I knew that to him I wasn't just a friend. It hurt, a bit, that I couldn't be more for him since I wanted him just as much as he wanted me. "I'd like you to come up," I said after a few moments. He wouldn't be able to come farther than the waiting room on the floor Simon was on, but having him there, knowing I had his support; I thought that might be enough for me. I hoped so at least.

"Simon's little sister though…. She can be a bit of a mess. She blames me for what happened to him, and I don't know how she'd handle seeing us together." I felt like I had to warn Caleb in case Cassandra went ballistic or something. It was already a lot to ask of someone I'd only really just met to come up with me. Dealing with Simon's little sister would probably prove to be too much for most people.

But Caleb just gave me a little smile that stretched his lips but didn't reach his eyes, as he said, "I'm just there as your friend. I won't hug or kiss you."

I nodded. That plan might work, I decided, as Caleb started to get out of the SUV and I followed after him. My steps were slow and my movements were jerky as we walked inside, but I managed to get us through the front door, past the chapel and the pharmacy, and up to the main elevators. The elevator was crowded, but after the first three floors where most people got off, it was a lot less so, and by the time we got to the tenth floor, only Caleb and I were on it.

The elevator doors opened and for a moment I was frozen there. Nothing had changed since the day Simon had been transferred there from the ICU on the first floor. The walls were still the same unsettling color of baby-puke green and a familiar landscape of ducks swimming in a mountain lake hung behind the desk where a woman stood to greet us. I didn't want to go out there. I would have been perfectly fine letting the elevator doors close on us and riding it all the way back down to the first floor where I would get out and go back to Caleb's car. I could buy him Mexican food from the place down the street to thank him for driving me down to Denver, and we'd be back in Thornwood by the time the evening news came on.

Only I couldn't do that. I knew that. I wanted to, but I had to officially say good-bye to Simon because if I didn't make my feet move, if I didn't get off the elevator, if I never went to his room and held his hand again… if I didn't get up the guts to do that today, then I knew I'd never have this chance again.

So I stepped out of the elevator with Caleb directly behind my right shoulder. He wasn't pushing me forward, but he was there, blocking my way out in case I decided to run. That might have been intentional, but maybe it wasn't. I didn't get a chance to ask him about it, though, because I saw Laura walking toward me.

She'd always been pretty, my once-upon-a-time future mother-in-law, but it looked like she'd dressed up especially for the occasion. Her sleek black dress, high heels, and chunky silver necklace made her look like she was entertaining clients at her law firm, not saying good-bye to her only son.

I felt extremely underdressed in my faded blue jeans and Thornwood Police shirt, but I couldn't do anything about that now. She hugged me before I could even open up my arms and then kissed my cheek. She even went so far as to smooth my hair back from my face.

"Look at you. Still as handsome as ever. Thank you for coming, Trent."

She kept her hands on my cheeks, and I wondered how she stayed so warm in such a cold, sterile-feeling hospital. I pulled slightly out of her reach so I could bring Caleb forward.

"And you brought some support. That's wonderful," she said before I could begin to introduce him. I saw her gaze go from me to him, and I figured I had a pretty good idea of what she was thinking. But she was classy and didn't say anything about me bringing a boyfriend to Simon's death.

I briefly touched Caleb's shoulder, but I would have much rather taken his hand and held it. I didn't want her to see me do that, though. Simon had been gone for five years, but this was still his mom and she'd always treated me well. "Laura, this is my friend

Caleb. He drove me here since I didn't think I'd be able to drive myself. Caleb, this is Simon's mom."

Her smile grew to one of acceptance and understanding with none of the previous judgment behind it as she took Caleb into her arms just as she had with me. He awkwardly patted her back, something I hadn't done since I hadn't been able to move.

"Nice to meet you," he said as they separated.

"You too, dear. I'm going to get some water. It's terribly dry in this hospital. Trent, I'll see you in the room soon."

It wasn't a question, so I didn't treat it like one. Instead I simply nodded and brought Caleb over to the waiting area. "There's hot chocolate and things here," I said unnecessarily. It was easy enough for him to look around and see the various cookie trays and beverage machines all waiting to be used by guests of the long-term-care floor.

"Thanks." Caleb sat down, then looked up at me.

There were so many things I could have said to him right then. I thought he was brave for coming here with me, sweet for being supportive when most people wouldn't have been, and sexy as hell in the just-a-bit-too-tight black tee he wore. "I'm glad you're here," I told him instead of any of that.

He gave me a slow nod and looked at someone just behind my right hip. "You should go see Simon. Laura is waiting for you."

I glanced over my shoulder at her and gave her a little wave. I'd be there soon; she didn't have to hover around waiting for me to join her family in Simon's room. "Will you be here when I get out?" I asked as I turned away from Laura.

He gave me a little smile and leaned forward over his knees. "Unless I find someone cuter." His voice was soft, like he didn't want to attract attention to us.

I wanted to touch him, to hold his hand, to feel the warmth of his skin beneath my fingertips. Just.... Anything to remind myself that he cared about me and wasn't going anywhere. He was my friend, and I needed him right then.

"I'll see you soon," I promised.

Caleb tilted his chin to the side before he shrugged. "Don't rush."

Nodding, I stepped back from him and headed toward Laura, who was still waiting for me with a glass of ice water held delicately in her hand. "He looks like a good friend," she said as we headed along a wide, deserted hallway.

"He is."

Three more doors to pass before we got to Simon's. I knew that physically I could walk that far but wanting to do so was a completely different story.

"Have you known him long?"

"A few weeks."

I saw her eyes widen a bit, but she didn't get to say anything about the short amount of time I'd known Caleb because by then we were walking into Simon's room, and I saw Cassandra sitting next to him in an ugly pink plastic chair, which reclined into something not quite comfortable but at least manageable. I'd fallen asleep like that with a thin hospital blanket over me in the first few weeks after Simon had been brought to the hospital. That had been back when I'd still held out hope of seeing him open his eyes again.

Cassandra had been crying; that was obvious by her red, puffy cheeks and bloodshot eyes. Simon's little sister had still been in high school when we met. She had to have graduated from college by now, but I wasn't going to ask her what was going on in her life or how she was. The first wasn't my business, and I could tell easily enough about the second. She was in hell—they both were—and I felt out of place just being there. Simon's dad had passed only the year before from prostate cancer and now his family was going to lose him too.

Cassandra stopped looking at me and went back to talking quietly to Simon as she rubbed his hand between her own. She talked about nothing and everything all at once. I heard about a kitten, how her roommate ate her favorite cheese, how the pizza wasn't nearly as good in Boston as she'd been told. I didn't interrupt her as I sat down across from her on Simon's other side. Laura tried to get me to sit up by his head, but I quietly refused. That was her place by her son. I was glad to hold his other hand. I didn't talk to him like Cassandra was doing, but not only because I didn't want to interrupt her.

I'd said everything I needed to say to Simon years before. I'd spent weeks at his side just talking to him, hoping for a miracle, begging him to wake up, wishing that my voice would somehow magically bring him back from wherever he'd gone. But nothing had worked, and the weeks had turned into months, which had slowly, painfully, bled into years. Laura had maxed out her credit cards, put a second mortgage on her house, and spent nearly all of Cassandra's college fund just to keep Simon in the best hospital in Denver. She'd needed a miracle too, but I was glad she finally decided he'd had enough and it was time to let him go. It wasn't the money that made her come here today. I knew she would have done anything she had to if she thought there was still a chance of Simon waking up.

I didn't tell her, but I was grateful she was going to let him go. We could all begin to grieve, to heal, and to move on. In some way I knew I'd probably always love Simon, but I didn't think it was good for them to be so tied to him like they were. I remembered rock climbing and sprinting through the forest around Thornwood with him. I chose not to remember him like this.

The man in the bed was thinner than my Simon had ever been. He probably could have gained twenty pounds and still not been a healthy weight. His lack of muscle also made him look small. Simon had never been built, but he'd been healthy and strong. They'd cut his hair, though, at Laura's request, about a month after he moved up to this floor. She said it was easier for them to manage. I remembered all the times she told him he needed a haircut. I knew he never would have shaved it all off, though, because when he was my Simon his hair had been down to the middle of his back and often braided. He'd been proud of it, and I could still remember the feeling of those long strands running over my chest when he was with me.

I rubbed my thumb over his knuckles and wished there was something, anything to let me know he was still around, that he knew I was with him. But I got no response, and maybe that was the most merciful thing of all.

The head of the department, Dr. Glen Fitzgerald, came in twenty minutes later. He'd been Simon's lead doctor for the last five years, and we all knew him pretty well. After I had to go back to work I called him every day for a while, hoping there was some change in Simon. Then my calls only happened weekly until once a month became the norm. I hadn't spoken to him in almost a year, but thankfully he didn't mention that detail as he gave each of us a soft smile.

"Laura, Cassandra, Trent, I'm glad the three of you could make it here today. Laura, you asked that something be said today, so I've invited Pastor Tom to come talk, if that's all right with you?"

Dr. Fitzgerald had a quiet way about him, something I'd always appreciated while on this floor surrounded by people who seemed to need the most comforting and patients who were completely helpless. Laura nodded and grabbed my free hand as tightly as she could. She laid her other over Simon's chest, where Cassandra placed her hand over her mother's. She couldn't speak between her tears but gave Dr. Fitzgerald a jerky nod.

I wasn't religious, and Simon hadn't been either, but Laura and Cassandra were, so I wasn't alarmed that she had asked for someone to come in today. Pastor Tom surprised me, though, because the first thing I noticed about him was the rainbow sash he wore over his dark gray suit. I stared at it for a good minute before I noticed his hand on my shoulder.

"Hi," I said. I licked my lips and squeezed Laura's hand when she nearly broke my fingers with her own.

"I know you two weren't much for churches, or God, and I understand why Simon felt that way," Laura told me softly. "But

I found someone who I think he would have liked to talk to. If he could have." Her voice broke on a sob, and I gave her a nod.

"I think we both would have liked to talk to someone like you sometimes," I told Pastor Tom honestly. It wasn't just that he obviously accepted our love; it was that he looked genuinely kind, and Simon had once told me the world needed more kindness in it. I tended to agree with him on that, even now.

"I'll leave my card with all of you. If you need to talk or want to come to the chapel to see me, I'm always available. If I'm not there, you can usually find me in the cafeteria by the chocolate chip cookies."

I managed a little smile at his words and took a deep breath as he stepped closer to Simon. "With your permission, I would like to say a prayer." Laura nodded and bowed her head.

Things were snowballing now, spiraling out of my control, though I'd never really had control around Simon to begin with. He was a firestorm in my life, and for nearly a year I'd felt like I was flying every time we were together. It seemed almost fitting that today would leave me with the same kind of whirlwind feeling.

Pastor Tom spread his arms a little, lifted his palms up, and looked right at Simon as if they were about to have a conversation before he and Cassandra lowered their heads. I kept mine up so I could watch Simon. Now that the time had come, I didn't want to look away from him at all.

"Dear Lord, we're here today to say good-bye to Simon Matthew Pritchard, a dearly loved son, brother, friend, and partner. Sadly I never had the chance to meet Simon before he came to stay at this hospital, but I'm told he was always happy, a good man, and the best kind of friend. Today we lose a special person full of compassion and love, and he will be sorely missed from this world. Lord, we ask you to please bless Simon today, to forgive him for anything he may have done in his life, and to welcome him into your arms so that he may be with you for all of eternity. Amen."

"Amen," I whispered brokenly, along with Cassandra and Laura. Cassandra looked over at me and for once I didn't see anger all over her face, or blame. For one short second she looked like she believed that I was hurting too, that I'd loved her brother as much as I said I did, and that I was sorry he spent the last five years of his life in this bed. I'd never wanted him to get hurt, never intended for him to fall. She never believed me in all these years, but right then it seemed like maybe she did. I hoped I was right, not because I needed her to believe me, but because I thought she needed to let go of blaming me for something that was truly an accident.

Dr. Fitzgerald stepped forward, along with two nurses, as Pastor Tom moved back. "When you're ready, we'll turn off the machines. Simon will be gone shortly after that. You're welcome to stay with him as long as you want. I'll make sure you aren't bothered."

"Thank you," Laura told him. "And you too, Pastor Tom."

He nodded, patted my shoulder, then stood quietly off to the side as Dr. Fitzgerald came closer. Laura whispered to him, because if she raised her voice any higher than that, it began to crack. I watched, with my breath held tightly in my chest, as Dr. Fitzgerald began turning off one machine after another. His movements were slow but precise, as if he didn't want to rush us in this process. I appreciated that.

The beeps of the machines slowly quieted and, after the nurses had checked him over and nodded to Dr. Fitzgerald, we were left alone with Simon. I continued to hold his hand, though I knew he was gone. He'd been gone for years. But still I couldn't stop touching him.

Nearly half an hour later, Cassandra was the first to get up from her chair. She'd been quietly crying, but as her cries had grown into loud sobs, I guess she'd needed to leave. When she didn't come back right away, Laura rose from her seat, kissed Simon on his forehead, touched me on top of my head, and then went after her.

Which left me alone with the man I'd once planned to marry, to spend the rest of my life with, to maybe even start a family with someday. We'd have a dog first, not children, though we'd talked about adopting them someday too. With his accident, though, everything in my life had been torn apart. I leaned forward and rested my forehead against his knuckles. I sighed and closed my eyes. I wasn't ready to leave, couldn't say good-bye to him yet. Knowing he'd been gone for years and being ready to never see him again were two completely different things. And I couldn't do the latter yet.

Someone came into the room and I didn't move. Whoever it was, I didn't care, but then I felt someone touching the back of my head, and I turned my head to see Caleb sitting down next to me.

CHAPTER NINE

Caleb

I WASN'T sure if I should have gone into the room, but once I saw Laura come out, and Trent hadn't come down the hall with her, I went in search of him. I kept my hand on the back of his neck as I sat down next to him in the empty chair.

"Hi," he murmured.

I forced a smile, even though I wasn't exactly comfortable being there. "Hey. Can I get you anything?"

Trent shook his head, then laid his cheek against Simon's hand. I didn't look at Simon and didn't really want to either. I wasn't comfortable around death, no matter who it was, and to add to that the person lying in front of us was someone Trent obviously still cared about. I know what he'd said. I'd heard him tell me he didn't still love Simon, but looking at his face and the tears in his eyes, I knew he either hadn't been completely honest with me, or maybe just not with himself.

And I couldn't bring myself to be mad at him for it at all. People thought they fell in love all the time. Hell, I'd thought I was in love with Paul. I might even have been. But I knew I'd never been in love with someone like Trent had probably loved Simon. I was jealous, and hurt, which made me feel like an asshole because regardless of anything else, including how much I wanted him, Trent was my friend, and right then he was hurting more than I knew I ever had.

I couldn't be stupid about this right now. When I was back home and by myself, I could figure this out. But Trent needed me to be with him and be as supportive as I possibly could be. And I'd do my best to be that for him. I could be friends with someone I wanted as badly as I wanted Trent. I hadn't tried before, but I could with him. I was sure of it.

He ignored my question, and I didn't ask him again. If he needed something, I'd get it for him. I'd ask someone if I couldn't find it, and if he wanted to be alone, I could do that too. I moved my hand from the back of his neck to his back, and finally I rested my hand on my thigh. A second later he put his hand around mine.

"I'm glad you're here."

I nodded. I could have told him thanks for letting me come with him, or that I was glad to be there. But neither of those would have been honest. I simply gave him a little smile and squeezed his hand.

We sat like that for at least another half hour without either of us saying anything. I didn't mind the silence, and I slowly became more comfortable being there. I could see where I stood in Trent's life and, in a small way, that was something I needed to know. Along with that, though, I guessed I could understand why he did what he did with all the guys in his life. He got his needs met without ever having to risk getting hurt. And he had been hurt, badly. I could see that now. Losing someone was probably one of the hardest things to get through in life, and he'd just lost someone he loved.

I was ready to leave the room long before he stood up. Some nurses came in as we were walking out, but Trent didn't stop to see what they were doing. We'd stopped holding hands as soon as we were out of the room, but I kept mine near his in case he reached for me and needed the support.

He didn't take me up on that offer until we were back in my SUV. "Where do you want to go to now?" I asked as his cold palm fit snuggly against mine.

"Hotel. I'll direct you."

That sounded just fine to me too. I was hungry, but once we were checked into the hotel, I figured I could find something to eat.

At the very least there had to be some Chinese restaurant nearby that would deliver to my room. When I pulled into the parking lot, though, I saw there was a grocery store right next door, and I gave a little sigh of relief. But at the same time I'd been kind of looking forward to some Chinese food. I couldn't find a single place to deliver to me in Thornwood and orange chicken was one of my weaknesses. Trent was a weakness of mine too, but I tried not to think about that as I slung my backpack, with just a few things that I thought I'd need overnight, over my shoulder.

I followed Trent into the hotel, we checked in, and then I watched him as he walked silently into his room. I shook my head and let myself into my room. It was small, but it smelled clean, and the sheets were soft once I'd stripped off the flowery comforter. I tossed my bag onto the bed, then headed back out to go to the grocery store.

Nothing really caught my eye in the aisles, especially since I didn't want to eat microwave popcorn for dinner and I had no way to cook anything else, and the deli counter was closed this late. I ended up with a tub of ice cream, a bag of plastic spoons, and a six pack of beer. It wasn't much of a dinner, but I hoped maybe it would help me tempt Trent into coming out to eat something later with me.

I knocked on the door to his room and gave him a smile when he opened it. "Hey. Snack?" I asked.

He'd been crying, not that I blamed him, and stepped aside to let me in with a little nod. Once I was in, he stripped off his shirt, and I tried not to stare as he stood in the middle of the hotel room in just a beat-up pair of jeans. And with how low they hung on his hips I could tell he wasn't wearing anything under them. I had to force myself to look away from the bit of dark hair I could see above the button of his pants.

I felt wrong for wanting him right then, given everything that he'd been through that day, but it was hard not to stare at him when he was showing off such perfect abs and nice arms. "I brought ice cream and beer," I told him as I took the ice cream out of the bag. I figured vanilla would be a safe choice. I preferred mint chocolate chip, or rocky road when I could find a really good brand that made it, but I hadn't wanted to eat the whole thing by myself. "It's vanilla. Hope that's okay."

Trent shrugged and sat down on the bed with his back propped up against the headboard with a pile of pillows. I joined him with the ice cream and beer. He turned the TV on to an old sci-fi movie, and we ate together. It wasn't all that filling, but that didn't really matter to me right then. I just wanted to spend time with him, to make sure he was okay.

"You're going to think I'm an ass," Trent said when we were nearly at the end of the pint of ice cream and I was on my second beer.

"For what?" He shook his head, like maybe he didn't want to tell me, but I wasn't going to let him off that easy, despite the shitty day he'd had. "C'mon, tell me."

He handed the ice cream to me, and I put it on the bedside table as he stretched out next to me on the bed. He sighed and I waited for him to start talking. We had all night. I wasn't going anywhere unless he kicked me out of his room, and I could have patience when I tried to.

But what he said when he looked up at me really did rock me pretty hard.

"I'm going out tonight. I won't tell you about it, and you won't ever meet him. I'll make sure of it this time. But I can't do this. I feel like I'm breaking apart inside, and I need to feel better." His voice was quiet, like he didn't want to say the words, like he was ashamed of them almost.

I just stared at him, a thousand thoughts rushing through my mind, none of them good. "Tonight?" I mumbled, not believing him. I'd heard him just fine. But Simon.... He'd just died a few hours before. I shook my head, not understanding how he could want someone else when he was hurting as badly as he was.

Trent narrowed his gaze at me. "Yes, tonight. Sex relaxes me. It makes me feel better. I'm telling you because you're my friend and because I didn't want you to worry about me."

"I'm worried about you anyway," I snapped at him.

He got off the bed and shuffled around a little, like he was anxious and uncomfortable.

"Look, I know you're hurting and upset, but don't go out and have sex with some random person tonight," I told him. I was angry at him, and I didn't understand what his point was in all of this. "Go for a run, get drunk, go punch something. But stop screwing people when you don't even know their first names." I jumped off the bed too and got in his face so he couldn't just walk away and ignore me.

"Don't you think I've tried those things? You think I started off by sleeping around years ago after the accident? I like having sex, and there's nothing wrong with what I do. I'm not asking for your permission here, Caleb. I'm telling you that I'm doing this, and I need you to let me go."

Shaking my head, I knew that wouldn't be good enough. He tried walking around me so I put my hands on his chest, stopping him in his tracks. "Don't go out tonight," I told him again.

"You can't stop me." He stopped struggling against my hands and just stood there with his hands around my wrists.

Licking my lips bought me a little time as I decided exactly what I wanted to say, and do. I could have let him go so easily. I would have been mad at him for doing something I considered to be stupid, but that could have been the end of it.

I didn't do that, though. Instead I shook my head and lowered my hands, with his fingers still wrapped around my wrists, to curl around his hips. "If you have to do this.... If you have to have sex with someone tonight, then do it with someone who wants you, has wanted you. Just one thing, make me believe that you want me too. We'll go back to being friends tomorrow, but for tonight be mine and let me be yours."

I thought he was going to tell me to fuck off, to push me away, to leave and do exactly what he wanted to do all along—which was to find someone who could be just a mouth and an ass for him to fuck and nothing more. I couldn't be that for him, but I didn't want to see him do that to himself either.

"I don't want to hurt you and you don't do sex like that," he reminded me.

I shrugged. I didn't, and he knew that. "I'll make an exception for you, just for tonight. If you brought someone back here, I'd be able to hear everything anyway since these walls are very thin. And I care about you. I want you. I want a relationship with you, if you're ever interested or want one, but I know you don't want that tonight. So this is what I can offer you." It was a compromise, and I didn't know how I'd feel in the morning after being with him. But if it kept him here, with me, then I'd do it. And it wasn't like I wouldn't enjoy sex with him. I knew I would.

He herded me back to the bed and laid me down across it with him on top of me. His mouth met mine, and he ran his tongue against my lips, seeking entrance. I gave in to him and sank into the bed a little more with his weight as he slid between my thighs and pressed himself against me.

Trent ran his mouth over my chin and down my jaw until I felt him resting his face against my neck. "I've wanted you since the first time I saw you," he murmured.

"In my house?" That'd been it for me too.

He chuckled, and I felt him lift up my shirt and press his palm against my ribs. "No. You were getting gas a few days before I stopped by your place. West side of town, little gas station. I heard you complaining that the pump didn't take credit cards."

I blushed as I remembered. "All of the pumps I was used to back home took credit cards, and I never had to go into the building. What were you doing out there?"

He pushed my shirt up over my chest, and I helped him get it the rest of the way off me. Once it had fallen to the floor, I wrapped my arms around his shoulders, loosely holding him against me. He was restless. I could feel it in the way he moved his hips against mine. But he wasn't insisting on rushing this, which I needed.

He kissed my collarbone and I sighed a little. I knew he probably didn't take this much time with the guys he was with, which made me special, I supposed. I wanted to be that to him, to matter to him, to be more than just friends.

"Putting out live traps for some feral cats the owner had seen around."

I nodded, because I guessed that seemed plausible enough. Really, though, as he brought his lips over my left nipple and slowly circled that hard point with his tongue, he could have told me that he'd been out hunting unicorns, and I wouldn't have cared.

When he bit down on my nipple, giving me a little pain to go with the tendrils of pleasure he was sending through me, I arched against his mouth. "Are you like this with everyone?" I gasped out as he licked my sensitive nipple before moving down my ribs.

"Like what?" he asked, as if he didn't know exactly what he was doing to me.

He didn't wait for me to reply as he kissed down my stomach and began unbuttoning my jeans. "Caring" was the best way I could describe him right then. He wasn't loving, I knew that. I'd seen Trent be loving when I'd found him with Simon. But he wasn't flipping me over and pushing into me without saying a word either, like I'd imagined him doing with the guys he was with on the nights when I couldn't think of anything but him no matter how hard I tried to focus on something else.

He lifted his head to look down at me from his place right by the button of my jeans. "Because I do care about you, Caleb. I can't give you the relationship you want, but I can be good to you tonight."

I nodded, accepting what he was able to do for me. It was something for me, and it kept him here, with me, where I knew he was okay. I tried not to think about what the morning would bring or how we'd go back to being friends after this. That didn't matter tonight when all I wanted was to chase away his pain and sadness in the only way he seemed to allow anyone to do. This would be enough for tonight.

Touching his hair, running my fingers through the long strands, I rested my head back on the bed and smiled as he undid my jeans and slowly unzipped me. I lifted my hips for him, helping him take my pants off, and was glad I'd worn flip-flops that were easy to remove as I lay naked in front of him.

Having only been with three people before, being naked with someone new came with a bit of nervousness. I was self-conscious, and also a bit modest, even though I tried to keep in shape the best I could. I figured with the number of guys he'd been with, that he didn't feel like that anymore. Curiosity had me asking him just to be sure, though. "Do you ever wonder what the guys think of you?"

He put his hand around my shaft, and I jumped a little at the feeling of him tugging me since I couldn't really see exactly what he was doing unless I grabbed some pillows to prop up under my head. I'd thought they were too far for me to grab, but once I reached out for them, I managed to hook just the edge of one, which brought another closer and soon enough I was able to watch him as he leaned over me.

"What do you mean? Like my personality?" he replied.

I shook my head and kept playing with his hair. "No, like your body. Are you self-conscious at all when you're with them?" Talking about the other guys who had been right where I was now, even as vaguely as I was, still felt odd in a way. But at the same time it also felt like maybe talking about them made it more real, like I was realizing where I stood with Trent and how this was going to be. It hurt, but it felt more realistic too. I knew sex with me wouldn't make him change his ways, though I kind of wished it would work out like that.

Trent ran his tongue up the underside of my cock, and I jerked back as I watched him. My fingers curled in his hair, seemingly on their own, and I quickly released him. No one had ever liked me doing that to them so I was pretty sure Trent wouldn't either.

"I tend not to care," he answered.

"You don't?"

He shook his head and slowly began running his hand the length of my shaft, all the way from my sac up to the head, just as I liked it. "I figure we're both there for anonymous sex, so what does it matter? I see their pictures ahead of time, typically from the neck down to their knees, and I have a photo of my abs down to my thighs posted. If they like what they see there and if I like what I see on them, the rest of it really doesn't matter. I don't spend the night looking at their faces."

He laughed as if he'd made a joke, and I felt a little sick. But I'd asked and I was getting the truth, so I couldn't exactly complain about it now that I'd heard it.

"I do feel a little self-conscious around you though," he admitted as he continued to gently stroke me.

I frowned and couldn't understand why that would be. "Really?"

He kissed my tip and gave me a little nod. "Yeah. I mean, you I'll actually be seeing tomorrow. We'll hang out, we'll watch movies. And I know you want me, but I also know I could be a bit bulkier and that I eat too many carbs sometimes." He shrugged and I had to laugh.

"You don't have to worry about that," I told him. I felt my face heat up instantly. "I like you just fine as you are."

"You do?"

I would have thought that was obvious, but I guessed to him it hadn't been. I took his free hand and gave him a little tug. "Come back up here please."

"You don't want my mouth on you?"

I bit my bottom lip at his words, and at the memory that suddenly sprang to life in my mind of the only other time his mouth had been anywhere near my cock. Of course I wanted that, but I also wanted to be kissing him too. And I couldn't have both. "I want to kiss you right now."

He shrugged and lay down on top of me again. Only this time he took off his own jeans first. Having him naked on top of me, with his cock rubbing against mine each time he took a breath, made me really warm as I just looked up at him. I pulled him down to me with a hand on either side of his cheeks and opened my mouth for him when he pressed his tongue against my lips.

He slid his hands against my hips as he pushed his tongue deeper into my mouth. I wrapped one of my legs over the back of his thighs and rested my hands on his shoulders. I knew what we were doing, what would come for me tomorrow, but it was so easy to forget about all of that while I lay there kissing him. I hadn't thought our first time would be in a hotel room, and not a great one at that. I'd pictured him lying across my bed with me riding him after we'd gone out to dinner. But even though we weren't doing anything like what I'd pictured for that special first time, I couldn't exactly say I didn't like this either. Just being with him and feeling his hair against my face as he moved his lips to my neck was nice. He gave me a light kiss, then another, before a quick nip followed them, causing me to yelp. Trent laughed and straightened up, but I wasn't too keen on letting him go so soon.

"You have to let me up," he said as he grinned down at me and rested his hand on my stomach.

"Why?"

He leaned down to lick my lips, and I kept him close with my hand on the back of his neck as I kissed him. He pulled away too soon, though. "I need to get a condom," he whispered against my lips.

"Oh." I blushed and quickly let him go, not realizing he was already at that point.

He went to his pants, pulled out his wallet, then took out a condom from one of the pockets. I tried not to think about him carrying around random condoms all the time. Maybe it was habit for him more than anything. Or maybe he'd known losing Simon was going to be hard on him, and he'd planned to meet up with someone, anyone, to ease the kind of ache that the experience must have been putting on him.

I didn't want to focus on that, but as he came back with the condom already spread over him and a little bottle of hotel lotion in his hand, my face must have given something away because he stopped before he got to the bed and just looked at me for a long moment. "What's wrong?"

I wondered if I should say anything, if it was worth mentioning at all, if I even had a right to question or judge him since I'd known who he was and what he wanted before getting into bed with him. "Do you always carry condoms on you because you plan to have hookups?" I asked bluntly. I did want to have sex with him, and I really didn't want to screw that up, but I wanted his honesty too. I wanted everything from him.

He looked almost indecisive as he stood there staring at me and I waited for an answer. As the seconds passed, I considered putting the sheet over me to hide myself from him, or even just getting dressed and going back to my room altogether. I could go to a movie, or I could ask for a new hotel room. I didn't have to be this for him, not tonight.

But the more I thought about just leaving him and letting him do whatever he was going to do without me there, the more I wanted to stay right where I was. This wasn't my smartest choice, but it wasn't my worst either.

"I have them on me so that if the possibility of having sex with someone comes up, I'm safe and I don't risk making a bad choice just because I'm in the moment," Trent told me.

I nodded. It was a good reason to have condoms on him.

"Do you want to stop this?" he asked.

I sat up on the bed and shook my head as I looked up at him. "No. I want you here with me. I want to help you get through this. I wish we were together, but this is okay." He didn't look convinced, and I forced myself to smile. I held out my hand for him, and he came closer to tangle his fingers up with mine.

"I do want you," he tried to assure me.

I nodded. "I know."

He looked sad and leaned down to give me a kiss. I reached up and cupped the side of his neck so I could brush my thumb over his jaw. The little stubble running along his cheek tickled the pad of my thumb. He pulled away and lay down next to me on the bed. "Maybe in time…." He shrugged. "I know that someday a relationship could be possible again. But right now…."

Trent shook his head, and I pressed my fingers against his lips. "I'm not expecting love, or even a relationship from you. I just don't want to see you meet up with strangers because you can't handle what's going on in your life right now. It's horrible, and I can't imagine losing someone I loved like you did. I want to be your friend, and I want to be more than that to you too. If you need sex to deal with your life, then… I guess I'm here. If you want me. For tonight."

That wasn't what I wanted from him, not really, but it was the most I was going to be able to get from him, and besides, it was more honest than anything I'd ever had with Paul, and that lasted me for years.

"I thought you weren't ready for another relationship so soon after your last," he said softly as I stretched out next to him with my hand still wrapped up in his.

"I'm not. And this, what we're doing right now"—I waved my hand between us—"this is completely different from anything I've ever considered doing before. But I can't stop wanting to be with you, and I don't want to think about you being with anyone else."

He frowned at me, and I got up enough to roll over on top of him so I was sitting on his lap. I leaned down over his chest and cupped his cheeks with my hands while I kissed him. I didn't want to hear him argue with me, didn't want to know how bad a decision this was. I didn't want to think I was letting him use me for sex, even though I knew that was pretty much what I was doing.

CHAPTER TEN

Trent

"YOU DON'T have to do this," I said as I put some pressure on Caleb's shoulders to push him off of me. He rose up, just a little, but it was enough for us to be able to talk again, which I really thought we needed to do.

He nodded and came back to rest his forehead against mine. I hugged him close and felt his chest rise and fall against mine with his deep breaths. "I know that," he said quietly.

"I've never cared about what any of the guys I've been with recently thought the next day," I told him as I smoothed my hands down his back. "But it's not like that with you." I stopped moving my hands at the base of his spine. I wanted to touch him everywhere, to grab him and fuck him hard into the mattress until we were both sweaty and exhausted. Maybe then I could actually think again without my thoughts getting jumbled with my emotions to the point that I could barely stand to be awake.

I stopped because he wasn't some nameless guy with a horrible username that I didn't remember the next day. He was Caleb, someone who had been there for me today and sat beside me while I said good-bye to a man I'd loved more than I ever thought possible. And here he was, telling me he wanted to be with me, that he was okay waiting, that he just didn't want me going out there and finding someone else to waste myself with. It was too much, and I felt bad for wanting him too but knowing I couldn't give him what he wanted. I would happily give him great sex. But more than that just wasn't going to happen right now. I wasn't going to say never, because I didn't know what would happen in the future, but tonight, in my hotel room, I couldn't give him anything more than my honesty and sex.

"Tell me you can handle this, that you won't hate yourself in the morning, that you won't regret spending the night with me," I demanded.

"Or what?"

I didn't have a way to back up my threat. I needed to go out, but I wasn't enough of an asshole to tell him that if he didn't have sex with me, I would go find someone else. I just needed him to be okay after this.

I shook my head and brought my mouth up to kiss him at the base of his throat. "Or nothing. I just want to still have you as my friend in the morning."

He looked a little relieved at that, and I moved my hands from his lower back to his shoulders so I could hug him again. I wasn't used to just touching people, to being naked with them, without having sex with them. It was nice, in a way, but I still wanted to be inside him.

"I'll be okay," he promised. I didn't know if he was sure of himself or not, or if he could really predict that, but I didn't question him any more as I moved my hands back to his hips, then brought them around to cup his ass. He ground against me as I moved my finger around his entrance, teasing him until he was gasping against my neck.

I turned him over so that I was on top again and pressed my hips against his until I felt him tremble under me. He spread his thighs, letting me rub against him as much as I wanted to as I moved my hand back to his entrance.

When I bit his neck, he moaned softly and I hoped it was enough of a distraction for him as I began to slowly stretch him open. He dug his fingers into my shoulders when I thought he was nearly there, and by the time I pressed the tip of my hard cock against him,

I had to hold him down with my free hand to keep him from moving around so much.

I laughed as he grabbed at me, seeming eager, and kissed him as I pushed my way in. He was tighter than I was used to and squeezed around me hard enough that I gasped out against his lips. I didn't have sex with guys like this, hadn't even looked one of my partners in the eyes while I was with them since Simon. Thinking about Simon in that moment hurt, and I tried not to let myself go there while I was with Caleb. But what I was doing with Caleb was a far cry from the fucking I normally did with people, and every second I spent being nice to Caleb reminded me of being with Simon. Things were done there; our time was past. It had been over five years ago, but now he was completely gone, and there was nothing I could do about it.

We rolled so that Caleb was above me again, and I didn't fight him as he began moving on top of me. I was still in him, but I didn't have the control I was used to having, that I was accustomed to needing. I pressed my hands against the tops of his thighs, holding on to him as he found a pace that worked for him. I watched him as he sought his pleasure, as he ground himself against me, as he gasped each time he took me all the way into himself.

He was beautiful in a way the guys I was normally with weren't, and I doubted if they could ever hope to be. I was used to hearing the foulest language from the loudest voices as I screwed them. That was normal for me. Sex was dirty and fast, and it was the most fun when I had all the power and control and the person under me could only hope to beg.

Caleb wasn't anything like those men. He was gentle with me and I knew I would have none of the usual scratch marks across my chest and back. I didn't know if this was his normal way or not, but I knew as he rested his face against my neck and told me how good I felt inside him that he was far too good for me.

And yet, as he held on to me and I gripped him as hard as I could, I knew he didn't see things that way at all. I could have shown him, and I was tempted to. I could have pulled out of him, turned him onto his stomach and fucked him as hard as possible from behind. He would have come; I know he would have, but it wouldn't have been as good for him as this was. And I didn't want to be cruel and treat him like just another hole for me to fuck, like everyone else was.

I wrapped my arms around his shoulders, holding him close, as I looked up at the ceiling and wished there could be another way for us. I couldn't give him what he wanted, but he didn't deserve the stain of what I could. And yet it seemed as if neither of us could stop being attracted to the other. I was hard just being around him, just sitting next to him, just hearing him laugh. That was new for me, and not entirely unwelcome.

He leaned back and I let him go to be able to run my hands down his damp chest and stomach until I circled my hand around his cock.

"Do you like this?" he asked.

I didn't like the uncertainty in his voice. I was hard and I was pretty close, but he must have been able to tell something was off about me. I nodded and hoped he didn't press me for more of an answer than that. To keep him from going down that train of thought, though, I began stroking him just the way he liked.

He leaned back again and braced himself on the bed by my knees. His stomach sank, his body shook, and then he bucked against my hand as he came over my chest. I licked my hand clean before I pulled him back down against me. I kissed him roughly as I shoved my tongue into his mouth. It was my turn, and I wanted to take him. I got him under me again and wrapped his arms around my waist as I slammed into him hard enough that I heard him gasp. I groaned as I felt his body clamp down around me. He felt great, and I knew I would want him again, but also that this couldn't happen again for us. Caleb was too good for me, too nice, too clean, for what I needed from him.

I leaned back and gripped his hips. He'd have bruises there in the morning, but I wasn't too sure he cared. His face was flushed, and he rocked against me each time I thrust into him. I wasn't used to being looked at, watched like he was doing to me, and having his eyes on me left me feeling vulnerable. I didn't enjoy feeling like that, and so I fucked him harder until he was crying out and dragging his fingers over my skin like he was in a frenzy. I buried my face against his shoulder and didn't look back at him again until I'd come.

I expected to see regret in his eyes, maybe even a bit of disgust, but he only looked exhausted. I slid out of him and took off the condom, tossing it into the trash can nearby. I wanted a shower, needed to feel the hot spray of water against my skin, but Caleb stopped me with a hand around my wrist. He stood up while I was looking down at him; then he kissed me, and I hesitated to put my arms around him, but it did happen eventually.

"Do you feel any better?" he asked when the kiss was over. He didn't pull away, though, and I didn't let him go.

I nodded slowly. "Yeah. Thanks." I didn't know what else to say in that moment. Normally I didn't have to say anything. It was enough that I'd come, that he'd come, that we'd had sex at all. I wasn't good at the after parts.

He gave me a little smile. "Good. I'm glad. So... a shower comes next, then?" Caleb moved away, and I followed him into the shower, still feeling completely out of my element. "How does this normally work with the guys you're with?" he asked lightly. I could hear the pain there, the hurt in his voice, and I shook my head.

"Don't do that. You're not one of them. And this wasn't like that." I turned on the hot water, as hot as it would go, then remembered I wasn't just going in for me, and I didn't need to scrub someone else off my skin. So I turned it down and checked the temperature before stepping under the spray.

"Then what was it like?" Caleb asked as he followed me in.

I shrugged, because I didn't have a good answer for him. What we'd done had been more intimate, more loving, than anything I'd done with anyone else in the five years since Simon's accident. I was hurting, and a bit scared, because I didn't know what to do next.

I couldn't kick him out, and I didn't lie down next to the people I was with. But I was pretty sure that's what would be happening after the shower, and I realized I wasn't as against that idea as I might have thought.

"Thank you for not going out," Caleb said as he unwrapped the paper from a tiny bar of soap and handed it to me. He had one for himself too and together we began cleaning ourselves off under the hot spray.

"You don't have to thank me for that," I mumbled.

"What was this like if it wasn't how you are with them?" Caleb asked again once he'd moved on to washing his short blond hair.

If he wasn't going to let it drop, I supposed I had to come up with a decent answer for him. Only I didn't have one. "More like making love, or what I remember of it at least." I didn't know if he'd heard me over the spray of the shower since I wasn't talking very loudly, and he might have had shampoo in his ears, but maybe, since he stopped washing his hair and just looked at me, maybe he did hear me.

"Did that still work for you, then? Or do you have to go out?"

I hated that he asked that. "I'm staying in." I washed myself as quickly as I could and wasn't even sure if I had all the shampoo out of my hair before I stepped out of the shower and grabbed a towel to wrap around myself. Once I was dry, I lay back on the bed, completely naked and not caring one bit. There wasn't a reason to hide myself, not now that we'd had sex.

Caleb came out a few minutes later with a towel wrapped around his waist and his hair still dripping wet. He lay down next to me, on his stomach so that he was looking at me while I lay on my back, and I looked at him.

"You don't seem okay."

I shook my head. I really wasn't. "I forgot what it was like to care about someone I was with," I whispered to him. I reached out and touched his arm with my knuckles. "It hurts in a way that being with random people doesn't."

125

He looked confused by that. "Why?"

I licked my lips and hoped he didn't hate my answer. "Because it reminds me of what I lost."

Nodding, Caleb sighed softly. "I'm sorry."

"Me too." I wished I could have given him everything he seemed to want from me. For whatever reason, this sweet, nice person actually wanted me to be with him. And I couldn't stop thinking about someone I'd lost five years before. I rolled over onto my side, put my arms around him, and then laid my head on the back of his shoulder.

I'm not sure how long I lay like that with him, but I must have fallen asleep. He was asleep too, with his soft snores coming against my arm in front of his face. As quietly as I could, so that I didn't disturb him, I got off the bed and went to the window. I didn't hide myself as I pulled the curtain a bit aside and looked up at the sky. I wanted to see the stars, the moon, the tall aspens around my townhouse. But all I saw were buildings and so much light that it seemed as if there were no stars anywhere in the sky above me. I shook my head and turned out the lights in the hotel room. Sitting in the darkness felt better.

Talking to my dad might have helped, but I dismissed that idea. I wanted to talk to Simon, but that was impossible. What I needed to do was get my head on straight and stop hurting Caleb, because it was pretty obvious to me that I was. Having random guys be mine for an hour or two was one thing, but I'd used Caleb for not only a stand-in for one of them, but also for Simon. As much of an asshole as I knew I could be, I was positive that treating him like that had been wrong.

I stayed up the rest of the night looking out the window and watching over Caleb as I thought things over. I was sure I shouldn't see him again, not like this. Being with him had been wonderful, and reminded me of what I'd been missing, but it had been a mistake. I was sure of it. Thornwood was too small to really avoid him, but I'd do my best. I'd be friendly, I decided, but being friends wasn't going to be possible. Not after the night we'd shared. He wanted more from me and maybe I did from him as well. But I wasn't ready for that and asking him to hang around and wait for me wasn't going to work either. I couldn't do that to him.

"Hey. Good morning," Caleb said as he sat up and stretched in bed. "You're already up?"

I nodded. "Yeah. I couldn't sleep."

"And you got dressed."

"You're very observant at eight in the morning," I joked. I'd been dressed since four, hoping he'd wake up early. I wasn't a morning person, but I supposed that changed when I hadn't really been to sleep.

He got out of bed and gave me a kiss. I let his mouth linger over mine and savored him for as long as I could before he straightened up again and headed toward the sink. "Want to go out for breakfast?" he asked before he started brushing his teeth.

"Sounds good. There's a diner not far from here."

"Give me ten minutes to shower and get dressed."

He sounded so excited, and I didn't want to discourage him. So I nodded, plastered on a smile, and waited for him to get out. I got another kiss on his way out of the shower and before he got dressed. He ran his tongue over the seam of my lips and fisted my shirt in his hand. If he wanted more, I didn't let him have it.

"Hurry up. I'm hungry."

He groaned and I smiled at him, a real one this time, because it would be so easy to just give in to him. He wanted me again, and I was ready to have him. But one mistake was enough for both of us. Caleb smiled, then quickly threw on some clothes from his bag that I'd brought over during the night. I checked us out of the hotel while he brought his SUV around the front.

We had breakfast at the diner down the street. It felt like a date, with him finding excuses to touch my hand and offering me bites of his omelet off his fork. We left and drove back to Thornwood, and I still hadn't said much to him.

"You okay?" he asked when we were back at his house.

"Yeah. I'll be fine." I gave him a little smile and hoped he thought I was only upset over losing Simon. That was a big part of it, but not really the full story.

We got out of his SUV, and I walked over to my patrol car. "So I'll see you later?" he asked. There was something there, hiding in his voice, and in the way he kept looking at me, like he could tell just how much I really was pulling away from him.

I wanted to joke with him, to tell him that of course he would see me since we lived in the same small town, but I could only manage a little nod. He stepped up to me, and I took him into my arms. I didn't kiss him, but I did hold on to him as tightly as I could before I got into my car. He was still standing in the driveway watching me when I drove to the main road.

CHAPTER ELEVEN

Caleb

I DIDN'T hear from Trent the next day, or even the next week. I saw him once, at the grocery store, but when I waved he didn't wave back. I'd left a few messages, probably a dozen texts, and two weeks after Simon's death, I was no longer just hurt and confused, I was angry at him. Luckily Dean, Nat, and Sam had come to stay with me and we had a fat, happy draft horse to foster.

"Dude, there you are!" Sam called as he ran up to me while I stood against the fence watching the gelding, Magic, graze. He was a lazy horse that was nearly as round as he was tall as far as I could tell. I was fostering him, but only for as long as Sam and his family were here, and only for as long as Sam was taking care of him. Luckily the kid and the horse had seemed to hit it off.

"Dude? No one says 'dude' anymore," I teased.

Dean and Nat were up at the house, doing what, though, I wasn't sure, but Nat was definitely in love with my house, though mostly my kitchen, I thought. She'd already made three of her pecan pies that I could never get enough of.

Sam bumped my shoulder and started to climb over the fence to sit on top of it. I stayed where I was. "He's an awesome horse. How long are you gonna keep him?"

"Long as you're here," I answered. He might have wanted to keep Magic beyond that time, but that wasn't happening. I looked back at the house to see if Dean or Nat were watching before nodding toward the horse. "Go get some lead ropes and his halter, and you can go riding." They'd been given to me by the rescue.

His eyes got really big as he jumped back off the fence and ran into the barn. His parents didn't mind that he went riding, as long as someone was watching him, but I had looser restrictions than they did on what Sam could do with the horse.

Magic would never be good for much more than pleasure riding; he was too old and too round, but he'd been a school horse, and according to Green Acres, he could handle anything. I'd been on him a bit, just to make sure he was safe, and I figured it was okay for Sam to get some time with him doing more than going around the pasture at a trot. Trotting was fine, but I grew up being a bit more wild on horses, and I remembered having fun with it, so I wanted to share that with Sam while Nat wasn't around to yell at me.

"Put the halter on him and get the leads on him like your reins. The rescue said he's fine bareback, and I've been on him like that, so that's how you'll ride too," I told him as he climbed back over the fence. There was an actual gate on the pasture, which I went through, but Sam was twelve, so I got why he refused to use the gate most days. Though, honestly, they'd only been with me for three days, and I'd seen him use the gate just to bring Magic through.

"Like this?" Sam asked.

I nodded and helped him tie them together so they didn't bounce against Magic's sides. "Now, get on him, get comfortable, but stay at a walk. We're going to do some fun stuff."

"At a walk?" Sam didn't sound convinced.

I smiled at him. "Yeah. Now get going before your mom sees us and we get in trouble for having fun." Sam was a good distraction, one I desperately needed to keep me from thinking about Trent and how he was avoiding me.

I helped him onto Magic's back, then took the lead rope reins from him while I led Magic around a bit. Sam looked disappointed in the pony ride, not that I blamed him, until I said, "Bring your legs up under you like you're a jockey. When you've got that down and you feel comfortable, I want you to kneel on his back."

"Won't I fall off?"

He looked so worried. It was pretty funny actually to see him uncomfortable with something since this had been the kid who couldn't wait to get into the water and go surfing the first time. This kid wanted to swim with great white sharks but was afraid of falling five feet off a horse. I had to laugh. "Maybe. But we're going at a walk right now and everyone falls off sometimes. You want to ride, you're going to fall off. Better you figure out how to fall correctly now than when you're galloping," I told him.

He didn't look convinced, but he grabbed some courage from somewhere and brought up first one leg and then the other. I was close enough that if he started to fall I'd catch him, but I doubted that he'd slide off. I was there more to make sure he didn't get hurt and that Nat wouldn't have another reason to yell at me. She'd already laid into me just that morning for washing all of my clothes together instead of separating them by colors and temperatures. If I did that, I'd never make a full load of laundry.

"How's this?" Sam asked when he'd gotten most of the way there.

I saw him clutching at Magic's mane and hanging on for dear life and wanted to challenge him some more. "Pretty good. You comfortable right there?" He gave me a shaky nod. "When you're ready, I want you to hold out your left arm. Straight out like an airplane." It was the arm closest to me and as he tried I was able to grab his hand and give him a little support until he wasn't so ready to topple.

"Now the other arm," I told him.

He shook his head, and I smiled up at him. "Sam, you're doing fine. Magic is the slowest horse I've ever seen, and you've got the balance you need from surfing. Put your other arm up. I'm right here."

"And if I fall?"

I rolled my eyes. He wasn't going to fall. I was right there, and I'd make sure he was fine. "Then I'll take you out for pizza. Just put your arm up."

Apparently that was a fair bargain because he brought his right arm up and after a minute I let go of his left one.

"I'm doing it!" he nearly shouted.

"I see that."

"This is awesome!"

I was glad he was so happy. "Yeah it is."

"Caleb!"

I cringed as I heard Natalie call me from the house. Sam quickly dropped his arms and went back to sitting on Magic with his legs down.

"I didn't do it!" I yelled back to her. "It was Sam!"

"Hey!"

Sam knew I was joking, though, because he covered his mouth to hide his laugh.

"There is a cute cop up here looking for you, so it better not be for my son!" Natalie yelled back to us.

I turned around, nearly tripping over myself, and sure enough saw Trent and Natalie standing on my back deck looking down at us. I lifted my hand to wave to him, and he gave me a little wave back.

"Kid, we gotta get this horse cleaned up," I said as I turned back to Sam.

"Why? I wanna go faster. We barely got started."

I shook my head and brought Magic to a stop. "Jump off. Let's go back up to the house."

"Are you in trouble? Is that why there's a cop here? Are you going to go to jail?"

"What? No. He's a friend." I rolled my eyes. This kid could be—

"Oooo. He's your boyfriend, isn't he?" Sam asked as he slid off Magic's back.

I gave him a glare, which only made him laugh as he ran out of the pasture, once again refusing to use the gate. I was left shaking my head and being very glad I didn't have kids of my own, as much as I adored Sam.

After I'd put away Magic's halter and lead ropes I headed up to the house, but Trent met me in the driveway before I could get there. "Leaving already?" I asked. I didn't know what he was doing there, or why he hadn't been returning my messages.

He shook his head and leaned against his patrol car. "Sorry to drop in. I didn't realize you had company."

"Friends from California who are visiting for a while," I explained.

Trent gave me a little smile and crossed his arms over his chest. "I saw Dean in the driveway and thought he was someone you were seeing before he introduced himself."

I snorted and shook my head, hoping Natalie hadn't heard that story. She could be a jealous woman when she wanted to be. "He's just a friend."

"I'm glad," Trent said.

I was still angry at him, as much as I was glad to see him again, so when he tried to come in for a hug I shook my head. "Nope. We need to talk first."

He didn't look that put off by my refusal. "I agree. Um... do you want to go to my place or do you want to talk here?"

I loved my house and was comfortable there, but I also didn't want Sam overhearing something he was too young to know about. "Let's go to your place. But I'll follow you."

"It's about a twenty-minute walk, even from the edge of town like you are here. I'm right in the center of Thornwood," he let me know, even as I headed toward my SUV.

"And if I get mad at you and want to leave, it'll be even faster to come back home with my vehicle." He didn't say anything to that as I got in my SUV and he went to his car. Natalie was watching me from the front door, and I gave her a wave before I pulled out of the driveway and followed Trent down the main street in town to a row of townhouses right by the grocery store.

"It's a lot smaller than your house," Trent warned me as we got out of our vehicles and headed toward a plain-looking townhouse near the end of the row. Trent's townhouse, like all the others on the street, had light gray siding and a dark gray roof. The only thing that really stood out to me was the faded police parking sign hanging on his front door.

"It's bigger than my apartment in LA was," I said as I followed him inside. "And cleaner too." Actually, his place smelled like fresh lemons. I figured it was probably a cleaner, but it didn't have any of the funky chemical smell that went with most of the cleaners I was used to. His front door opened up to a living room with one couch in it, like mine, but his was a lot newer. I saw a small kitchen to my left and two doors, one of them for the bedroom and the other for the bathroom, I guessed, but I didn't ask.

I was still too mad at him for ignoring me.

He tried to hug me again after closing the door behind me, and this time I let him. It felt good to be in his arms again, to be held, and it reminded me of the night we'd shared. As those thoughts sprang to life in my mind, I pulled away, and he let me go.

"How've you been?" he asked as I leaned against the wall next to his couch.

I shrugged and stuffed my hands in the pockets of my jeans. "Busy. How's your sex life been?" I was being blunt and I could have been nicer, but I didn't see a reason to be. He'd hurt me, and I had a right to be angry with him for that.

He blanched a little, and I felt slightly better at knowing he wasn't unaffected by my anger. I needed to know that, needed to see that what I thought of him and what I said actually mattered to him on some level.

"Quiet," he admitted. I waited for him to tell me more, to let me know just how many guys he'd fucked since me. I wanted that kind of information because if I knew, if I heard the numbers, then

I'd know for sure I hadn't mattered and maybe I could have started to give up whatever feelings I had for him.

But he didn't say anything more than that, so I asked him directly. "How many since me?"

"Caleb...." He shook his head and came closer to me. With the wall against my back, I couldn't move away, but when he put a hand on my hip and rested his forehead against my neck, I didn't move to touch him. I turned my head away and looked toward his front door. I shouldn't have come here. Being alone with him, when I still wanted him so badly and cared about him far more than I should have, was not a good idea in the least.

"I'd like to know the number," I said. He pressed his mouth to my neck, and I shut my eyes.

"Why? What would knowing do for you?"

Trent lifted up my shirt and pressed his hands to my stomach. This wasn't a brief touch at all. Instead I felt the warmth of his palm completely against my stomach, and I stood there, absolutely unsure of myself as my resolve to be angry with him, to hate him almost, began to slip away.

"Because I want to know how little I meant to you." It was the truth, and all of my hurt and anger wrapped up into one little sentence.

I pressed my lips together as he pulled his mouth from my neck and used his hand to turn my face toward him. I looked at him, waiting for an explanation. But instead he kissed me. I didn't open my mouth for him, didn't even think about it, and after a few minutes of trying to get me to kiss him back he stopped. Then we were just staring at each other again.

"You know what I'm like," he reminded me, as if it was my fault that we'd had sex and then he hadn't called or texted me back.

"You said we would be friends afterward," I countered. He put his other hand on me too, both of them on my stomach, right above the button of my jeans. "I called and texted you, and you didn't say hi back once. That's not what friends do."

He scrunched up his face, like he was upset about what I'd said, and I expected him to move back, since I clearly wasn't into what he was offering, but he moved his hands lower so that he was cupping me through my jeans. I lifted my eyebrows at him. "Really? Did you bring me here because you thought we'd ever be having sex again?"

This time he did stop touching me, and as stupid as it was, I wished he hadn't. He braced his hands on the wall on either side of me, holding me there in front of him. If I bothered to take my hands out of my pockets, I could have touched him too, but I knew where that would lead. I wanted him, and he clearly still wanted me. And if I got to touch him, then we'd end up together again. We might not even make it to the bedroom. Part of me didn't see a problem with that, and it was at war with the thoughts in my head about how hurt I was and how angry I'd been at him for not calling me back. It was such a simple thing, to want an answer to a text message.

"I was worried about you," I told him as he leaned his head against my shoulder. I let myself do the same to him. He smelled like pine trees, like the forest that grew around Thornwood. I closed my eyes and relaxed by a few degrees. It wasn't much, and I definitely hadn't forgiven him for anything. But with him here in front of me, his warm breath on the side of my neck, it was hard to be as mad at him as I had been.

"I know. I got your texts."

"You didn't say anything back."

He sighed and kissed my neck. "I'm sorry."

That really didn't do anything to calm my anger. He was sorry, which was great and all, but seriously, what the hell?

"Tell me how many guys you've had sex with since me." I didn't like repeating myself, and I should have just let it drop and figured it was anywhere from one to ten, maybe, but I wanted a real answer.

He didn't answer me at first, and I thought I'd have to ask him again. But then he did. "None."

136

I frowned, because he had to have been lying. "Yeah, right."

Taking his phone out of his pocket meant moving away from me, and I wished he hadn't. But then he showed me the app on his phone with all the guys he'd either had sex with or wanted to. "The star in the corner of their profiles is red if I've been with them recently. It's supposed to be fun, like we were hot together or something stupid like that."

He logged in, then handed it to me. I didn't need stars on an app to tell me he hadn't been on it recently, though. "Says here you have forty-two unread messages and haven't logged in for fifteen days." It was nosy of me to go through his messages, and I should have just given him the phone back. But I wanted to know what the guys who wanted him said because I was in that group too. I may not have met him on some cheesy hook-up app, but I'd been just another man in his bed. I'd known that when we were having sex, and the first day afterward had been hard. But it would have been a lot easier if he hadn't completely shut me out.

"This guy says he misses you," I told him. I felt disgusted with myself just looking through the messages, but it was hard to turn away and stop reading them once I started. "This one wants you again."

Trent shrugged and reached for the phone. I handed it back to him without a fuss. It wasn't any of my business what he did. We'd tried to be friends, and it hadn't worked. Now he was just some guy I desperately wanted, and had honestly really liked, but knew I wouldn't be having again.

"These are the kinds of idiots I have sex with," Trent told me.

"Thanks for lumping me in with them," I snapped defensively.

He quickly shook his head and went back to putting his hands on me, this time on my hips. He still went under my shirt, though, and ran his thumbs over the band of my jeans. It was getting harder to stand still with my hands in my pockets instead of touching him too. It would have been so easy to give in, to say screw it and just have sex with him and figure it out in the morning. But I was better than that, and stronger than that, and I was worth more than just someone for him to fuck when he was having a bad day.

"That's the problem. You're not like them. Not to me." His voice was soft, and a second later he kissed me. I couldn't keep fighting him, not that I'd ever really been that good at it, and I kissed him back. But I refused to touch him. He moved his hands around to cup my ass through my jeans, and I opened my mouth a little for him. When he pushed his thigh between my legs, rubbing against my cock as he had me pinned to the wall, I flicked my tongue between his lips.

I didn't think about what he'd said, or question him about it either, as my will slowly cracked. I brought my hands out of my pockets and rested them on his chest. He put his hands under each of my thighs and lifted me up. I slid my legs around his waist and didn't stop him as he pushed against me, letting me feel every hard inch of him.

Wanting him wasn't the problem; it was how I felt about myself afterward that was. If I could just be one of his anonymous hookups, then I could have easily given in. I probably wouldn't have had on my clothes shortly after arriving. But I wasn't like that, couldn't be, and the only way I was going to let Trent have me again was if there was something more between us. I didn't need a ring, or even a promise of years to come, but I did need commitment. I'd been the other person, and I wasn't doing that ever again.

I pulled my mouth away from his before we could go any further. "Trent, enough. Stop." He slowly let me down and hung on to me until I moved away from him.

"I can't be someone that you just have sex with. I'm sorry. I wish I could, because then things would be a lot easier between us, but I'm not like that," I said as I began backing up toward his door.

He took my hand, stopping me before I could get away from him and back to my house, where I was usually much saner. "I didn't bring you here to have sex with you," he said.

"Really?" I didn't believe him for a second.

He gave me a little grin. "Okay, maybe a little. But mostly I just needed to talk to you. And then I had you here and we were alone and I can't not touch you when we're alone." He shrugged and pulled me toward him. I came and he let go of my hand. "Talk to me for a bit?"

I nodded. "Sure." I could manage to talk to him for a little while without wanting to yell at him. Probably. Wanting to have sex with him was always there, but yelling at him was something I had wanted to do often enough to him too in the past few weeks. He was frustrating in a way few people had ever been for me before, Paul included.

We sat down on his couch and our hands seemed to come together on their own without me wanting it. But I didn't pull away. It was good to hold his hand, to feel his rough palm against mine, to lace our fingers together as we sat quietly in his living room. I didn't want to start talking first, and he didn't start either. But one of us had to.

I laid my head down on the back of the couch and looked up at the ceiling. "Did you not have sex with any of them because you didn't have a bad day since we last spoke or because you found somewhere else to get your needs met?"

"Neither. What makes you madder, that we had sex or that I needed some time to myself after?" he asked.

He hadn't given me much of an explanation, but after asking him the same question repeatedly, or what felt like the same question to me at least, I didn't really want the answer anymore. That wasn't true. I did want the answer. I wanted it a lot. But I wasn't going to keep pushing him if he so clearly didn't want to talk about it.

I turned my head to glare at him, but he wasn't looking back at me, so I wasn't sure if he noticed it or not. "I was mad, and still am really, that you just cut me out like you did to Eli and every single one of the other guys you screw and never talk to again. I didn't expect a lot from you, but I did need to know that I wasn't like them, that we were friends who had sex once when you needed someone to be there for you and that we would be friends again after."

Trent nodded, and I felt him squeeze my hand.

"That wasn't too much to ask," I added.

"I know. And I'm sorry about that. I needed to have some time to think."

"About what?" I asked.

He shrugged and turned his face toward me. We were so close in that moment our noses were practically touching. I could have kissed him if I'd wanted to.

"When Simon fell, I felt broken apart. I'd never lost anyone before. And he wasn't really gone, but at the same time he was. And I got used to thinking of him like that. Then anytime I felt needy or like maybe I wanted to try a relationship again, I'd go out and find someone to have sex with. I don't mind what I did, and it reminded me I could still get my needs met without having to care about anyone beyond making sure they had a good time with me. I never felt dirty or like I was using them."

I frowned, not entirely sure where he was going with this, because I didn't want to know any more about why he had sex with so many people like he had. I kept asking though, like I couldn't help myself.

"But with you I realized I had used you. And I'd used you not only to meet my own needs and get rid of the pain I was feeling, but also as a stand-in for what I remembered having with Simon. I kissed you, I held you, I fell asleep with you. That doesn't happen normally."

I was starting to feel sick and tried to get up, but his hand in mine stopped me from being able to. "Let me go," I told him as I pulled my hand out of his. I headed toward his front door while shaking my head and wondering why the hell I'd ever thought coming to his home was a good idea.

"Caleb... wait."

I stopped and turned with my hand on the doorknob. "Why? You just told me that being with me was like having sex with your dead ex. That's the worst thing I've heard in a long time, and I don't think I can hear anything more from you right now. I'm going. I have to."

CHAPTER TWELVE

Trent

"THAT'S NOT what I meant—" I tried to explain, but he was already out my front door and heading back to his SUV with the door slamming behind him. I sighed and sat down heavily on the couch. "Fucking perfect."

My phone beeped, letting me know I had a message. I thought maybe it was from Caleb, hoped it would be actually, as improbable as that would have been, but instead it was from some guy on the app. I deleted it without a second thought.

Come back. I texted him.

Caleb isn't available right now as he currently wants to kick you in your dick.

I smirked and shook my head. Of course he was angry. I hadn't explained things properly to him at all, so I had almost expected this from him. But it still hurt more than I realized it would to have him walk away from me like that.

Let's talk.

We tried that. It didn't work out so well. Also, I'm not Simon. You got weeks away from me. Give me that too.

I wanted to argue with him, to tell him that of course I knew he wasn't Simon, that I hadn't even been saying that about him. But when I tried calling his phone a few minutes later, it went straight to voice mail.

With a groan I tossed my phone to the other end of the couch. But I had one last text to send him before I really gave up, so I grabbed my phone again and texted him. *Give me one more chance. Please.*

I DIDN'T expect to hear back from him right away, not after the last text he'd sent. It took him four whole fucking days to respond to any of my texts. I kept asking him for another chance, for one more time from him. I promised to behave myself but after four days of not hearing from him it was damn hard not to go over to his house and bang on his front door until he came out to talk to me. *Can I have one more chance? Just one?* I miserably tried texting him again, sure he would ignore it just like all the others I'd sent him over the previous week.

To do what? was all he said a minute later.

I was sitting at my desk at work after having returned from a shoplifting kid call at the grocery store. The kid had been an easy call, which I was getting tired of my dad sending me out on after Simon's death, like I needed to be handled with kid gloves instead of being allowed to work like I normally did. But I'd remembered to grab myself some chips for lunch while I was there, so that was something, I guessed.

To be your friend. I texted back. I wanted him in my life and a friend was better than nothing.

He texted me back almost immediately. *No. I have enough friends right now.*

Well, that was unexpectedly harsh.

Okay.

With my appetite suddenly gone, I tossed the rest of my chips into the trash and shook my head. Well, fine, then.

If you ever think you can have an actual relationship, let me know.

That text surprised me. I didn't know if I could. I didn't know if I ever wanted to get back to that place of being with just one person, of caring about them so much that I willingly gave them a huge part of myself. Being in love was terrifying, and now that I'd been through it, and lost it, I didn't understand why people wanted it so badly. I hurt every day because Simon wasn't with me anymore.

Someday I knew that I would probably have to move on, to welcome someone new into my life, but at the same time I didn't see why I had to either. My dad wanted to see me settled down, but being with someone like that wasn't all it was cracked up to be. I didn't want to let Caleb go so easily, though.

I rubbed my hands over my face as I tried to figure out what to do about him, and also my feelings for him. Saying good-bye completely to him wasn't an option. But neither was jumping headfirst into a relationship either. *Can we try a date on Saturday? I'll take you out.*

Counteroffer. You come over here. Natalie is a great cook and has been insisting on meeting you.

I remembered Natalie, and her extremely good-looking husband, from his place. I was surprised they were still there, though. *Sure. Time?*

Six.

See you then.

I considered putting in a smiley face or some other crap but decided against it right before I sent the text off. We weren't children, and I didn't need a smiley face to show him I was glad he was willing to give me another chance. Whether I deserved it or not, though, was something that had yet to be decided.

I was at Caleb's house right on time. I'd even worn a pair of my best jeans. But I got distracted before I could get to the front door by watching a kid trot around on the draft horse that was barely bigger than a pony Caleb had in one of his pastures.

"Hey," Caleb said, coming out to greet me as I stood on the path. "Dean said you were out here."

"Hi. Sorry. Is that a horse or a pony?" I asked.

Caleb shrugged. "Green Acres called him a draft horse mix. I think they were exaggerating on his height in calling him a horse, but for a kid he's a good size."

"I'm glad you decided to foster for them, even after knowing about me and the guy from the sanctuary, since there are a lot of horses that need help." I saw him flinch, and I cursed myself for mentioning him. It was stupid, and I shouldn't have done it at all. Caleb didn't need the reminder that I'd been with more guys than him. "I'm sorry," I said with a sigh.

He nodded and turned to glance up at the house. "We should head up before Natalie sends Dean to come bring us in. Or before she comes after us herself."

I wanted to get to know his friends and the people who were important to him. But I couldn't help feeling like there might be something else going on. "Did you want to be here instead of at my place for any reason?" It wasn't meant to sound like I didn't want to be there, so I hoped he didn't take it that way.

"Yeah. I didn't want to be alone with you right now," he quietly told me as we started heading up the narrow path that went from his driveway to his front door.

That stung a bit, but I probably deserved it. "Any reason?"

"Can't have sex with you when there are other people around." Caleb was being blunt, and honest. I liked that about him.

"Probably best." He shot me a look, and I nodded to his unspoken question. Hopefully I'd guessed it correctly, though. "As much as I want you in every position and in every room of your house, on each and every surface, I don't want you to be angry with me anymore. You've got every right to be, because I did use you, but I'd rather not fight with you anymore."

He gave me a weak smile. "I'd rather not either." We were almost to his front door, and I wished we could talk instead of going inside. "I like you a lot, and trying things again, but slower, would be nice. I'd need commitment from you, though, and you can't do that. Until you can, then I don't know what to tell you."

I understood where he was coming from and knew I could try that. But I was pretty sure that just trying, and promising that I'd be committed to him, weren't going to be enough. He wanted a relationship, and he deserved one too. I couldn't offer him that. Not yet at least.

"Let's go inside," he said when I hadn't replied to him.

"Okay."

His house smelled delicious, and I could have spent the rest of the afternoon sitting at his island and just soaking in the smells of pecan pie, orange-glazed ham, real mashed potatoes, and collard greens.

"So, how do you know my Caleb?" Natalie asked me right before I managed to stuff another bite of her rolls into my mouth.

I stopped buttering it for a second to answer her. For some reason Sam was watching me intently, like my answer absolutely mattered to him, while Dean kept eating. Caleb met my gaze, briefly, before putting more mashed potatoes on his plate.

"We met when I came to check out the new person in town. It's a small town, and Caleb made up quite a bit of the gossip for the first few weeks because of this big house and not having a family. My dad is the one who first sent me over to make sure he wasn't a serial killer with bodies in the basement actually."

Caleb snorted and I smiled at him. "I didn't know that part. Did your dad ever approve of me moving here, then?"

I shrugged and was glad he returned my smile. "Jury's still out. But no one has gone missing from here lately, so he probably figures you're okay and just some crazy rich guy instead of a crazy, murdering rich guy."

Natalie cleared her throat and took a drink of the white wine we were having. I didn't miss the look she gave Caleb, though, as we continued eating. She even nodded at me while trying to get some message across to him. I'd be asking him about that exchange between them later for sure.

Pecan pie with ice cream was amazing after dinner, and when everyone else took a second slice, I was glad I wasn't the only one who needed one. Dean was still the most ridiculously good-looking black man I'd ever seen, but I wasn't fumbling over myself anymore like I had been when I'd first met him and thought he was someone Caleb had started dating. Thankfully Caleb had been down at the pasture then.

After dinner Caleb took me down to the barn, and I felt like I was ready to talk to him. "I like your friends," I told him as we walked down the trail.

"Thanks."

I offered him my hand, by brushing my knuckles against his, and was surprised that he put his hand in mine. We didn't stop at the barn, like I thought we would; instead we went into the woods behind his house. I was glad he was making use of all the government land around him. The dense and beautiful woods were wonderful to walk through. "I need you to know that I'm not Simon," he said when we'd managed to get pretty deep into the forest.

"I do know that," I told him. I felt instantly defensive and had to take a breath before I screwed this up with him any more than I already had.

He stopped walking and found a dry bit of moss to sit on as we leaned against a large pine tree. Still his hand was in mine, and I hoped he didn't take it away from me anytime soon.

"You don't, though, not really. At least I don't think you do," Caleb pressed.

I turned to look at him, waiting for him to continue with whatever he was going to say. But I wasn't going to tell him that right away. He let go of my hand, and I was instantly disappointed by the lack of contact with him, but then he got up. "Open up your legs."

My mind instantly went dirty, I couldn't help it. I grinned up at him as I started thinking about him on his knees in front of me, my cock buried deep in his mouth, the head pressing against the back of his throat as I fucked him. "Why?" I was already getting hard and moved my hand to my stomach, right above the button of my jeans, so I could open my pants and make things easier on him.

"Just do it." He rolled his eyes, and the grin never left my face. But once I'd opened my thighs for him, he just sat down between my legs and leaned back against my chest. I swallowed thickly, both because I didn't want him to feel how hard I was, and also because this wasn't something I did, ever.

But I wrapped my arms around his waist and rested my chin against his shoulder anyway. His hands came over my arms, and I tried to relax and not think about how good it felt to hold him, to have someone I cared about in my arms again. In my mind I just kept trying to remind myself not to say anything stupid, to not screw things up with him. Again. I didn't know how much I wanted from him, how far I wanted this thing between us to go, but I did know I wanted another chance to show him that I could be a decent person, that we could be good together, and that I knew how to treat him well and not to selfishly use him like I had.

His phone beeped, and he let go of me with one of his hands to pull it out of his pocket and check it. I saw a picture of a guy holding his hard dick and a message saying *I need u*. I tried not to tighten my arms around him or give in to the hypocritical jealousy I was feeling in that moment at the thought of Caleb with whoever it was that had sent him the text. He wasn't mine to get jealous over, but at the same time I didn't want him to be with anyone else. Especially not someone who couldn't take the two extra seconds to type out "you" on their phone.

"Do we need to go back?" I asked. I hoped I didn't sound like I'd looked over his shoulder at his phone, but it had been kind of hard to avoid seeing it too.

Caleb shook his head as he deleted the text, and I felt a wave of relief go through me. He put his phone back in his pocket before answering me. "Not yet, though we can't stay out here all night either. I'd get too cold. But that was Paul. He's in Denver for a meeting and has been trying to get me to go see him."

"Are you going to?" I hoped his answer was somewhere along the lines of "hell fucking no" but if he said he was going to, I knew I'd have to find a way to be okay with that. It wasn't like we were dating or like I had any kind of claim to him after all.

"No."

I smiled against his shoulder and hoped he couldn't see how happy his decision had made me. "Okay."

"He's an asshole who sleeps around."

Caleb sounded so bitter saying that, and it made me flinch because I slept around too. "Like me," I couldn't help saying.

He was quiet for a while as he curled his fingers over my arm, softly tickling me. "No, not really like you. I knew you were with other people before I decided to get into bed with you. I made that choice freely. With Paul I thought I was the only man he was with. I knew he was married, but when he told me he loved me, I believed him. After coming here I found out that wasn't true. You were always honest with me, so no, you're not like him."

"But it does bother you that I've been with a lot more people than you have." I knew the truth of that and didn't need him to confirm it for me.

He shook his head, though, surprising me. "That's not really why. It's more that you don't want anything more than that. I want you for more than sex. I like how we are right now. If I could have this more often, then I would. But I can't have this and know that you're also with other people. When you have a bad day, you need help, and I may not always be here to help you through that. I don't want to be cheated on by someone I care about as much as I'm starting to care about you."

I kissed the side of his neck and held him a little tighter. "I've never cheated on anyone, but I do see what you're saying. I don't know what I could do that would make the pain go away as well as sex. I need to feel completely drained of everything to feel right again."

"Maybe feeling right immediately isn't the answer," he quietly said.

"I don't know what you mean."

"Maybe you need to deal, to go through the pain and actually process it rather than having sex until you can't feel anymore." He

149

shrugged, and I tried to fully consider what he was saying. "I don't know what you're going through. I can't even imagine that, and I want to be here for you, but I can't have sex with you, not again, without us being in a committed relationship, and I don't think I can be friends with you either." He shook a little in my arms, and I kissed his shoulder.

"I know," I said gently. "I want more than friends with you too. I don't think I remember how to be in a relationship, though, and I don't want to do anything else to hurt you."

"Well, we could start with a date," he offered.

Nodding, I remembered dates. I even remembered the kind that didn't come with a promise of sex in the hotel room I'd already paid for before ever meeting the guy. "Movie?" I asked.

"And dinner out. So that I'm not tempted by you."

That made me smile. "I tempt you?"

He laughed and turned to kiss my cheek. "You have no idea."

A wicked idea came to me, and I nuzzled the side of his neck as I lowered my hands until my fingertips were just barely brushing the front of his jeans. "I'd love to have you right here with my cock buried in your ass and my hands in your hair. Your nails would scratch down my back as I bit your neck and fucked you into the leaves until you were crying out."

He was panting by the time I was done describing my current fantasy with him, but instead of giving in to me, he shook his head and swallowed thickly. "See, that's the issue right there. You're too fucking hot."

I nipped at his neck and felt him start to tremble against me. "Trent...," he groaned. I could tell his resolve was starting to crack, and I moved my hand lower to the front of his pants and gave his cock a hard squeeze through his jeans. But he put his hand over my wrist, stopping me before I could do more. "Date first."

I was disappointed, and I must not have been very good at hiding it either because he laughed. "You're such a baby."

"Can I have a kiss at least?" I asked.

He rolled his eyes, but he was still smiling at me. "As long as you know the kiss won't lead to sex tonight."

"What about if it leads to me sucking your cock and making you come?"

His eyes got wide, and I heard his breath hitch. "No. Can't do that."

"You want to, though." It didn't take a genius to figure out how much he just wanted to say yes to me, and if I kept pushing him on it, I was sure I could get him to do just that.

He nodded and brought my hand back up to his stomach, a good distance away from his cock where I really wanted to be touching him. "Of course I do. What sane person wouldn't want your mouth on them? Fuck, I've been thinking about you sucking me off since the first time you found me on my back in my bed and cleaned me off with your tongue. No one had ever watched me come before, and there you were, refusing to go away, just quietly staring at me like I was giving you some private show."

"The best kind of private show," I murmured against his neck. I was fully hard and sure he could feel me pressing against the small of his back.

"But it doesn't mean it's going to happen tonight."

I groaned at his resilience. "I should stop trying, then."

"Yes, please. One date. We'll try dating… we'll try this between us again. Maybe then I'll find out some stuff about you, and we can actually get to know each other."

I frowned. I couldn't remember the last time someone had wanted to know something about me. Everyone in Thornwood seemed to know more about me than even I did sometimes. "Like what?"

"Where were you born? Here in Thornwood?"

That was easy enough. "Denver. My parents were at the zoo when my mom's water broke. If the paramedics hadn't arrived first, my dad says she would have had me right there by the zebras."

He chuckled and I smiled at him. "You?"

151

"Lexington, Kentucky. My mom wasn't at the zoo like yours, or anything nearly as exciting. She was at home, called my dad back from work at the job site he was doing construction on, and they went to the hospital."

I nodded. It was good to find out some things about him. I wanted to keep going, not just because I wanted to get to know him more, but also because it delayed us going back to his house. I liked his friends, and thought Natalie was a great cook, but I also wanted him alone with me as long as I could possibly keep him there.

"Where are your parents now?"

"I don't know. My sister is still fairly close to them, but they aren't people I talk to anymore. She used to tell me how they were doing, but since they don't care about me, or don't seem to since I came out to them, I try not to think about them."

"I'm sorry." I couldn't imagine being cut off from my family like that, or being rejected like he had. I nuzzled the side of his neck until he laughed. I hadn't intended to make him laugh, but I was glad I could.

"That tickles."

"Good. Where else are you ticklish?"

He snorted and shook his head at me. "No way in hell am I telling you that."

"Why not?" I asked with a pout.

"You can already make me want to get naked the second you walk into a room. You really think I'm giving you even more power over me?"

I grinned at that idea. "Totally naked?"

Caleb was smiling even as he rolled his eyes at me. "Yes, totally naked. Maybe even on my knees for you."

"Fuck you're a tease."

He pulled out of my arms, and sadly I wasn't fast enough to stop him from getting up. "Not nearly as much as you are. C'mon, we should head back to the house."

"Already?" I protested. The sun was nearly setting, so I knew we should get going, but I could also see lights from the cabin in front of us, so getting back in the dark wouldn't have been impossible either.

"Yes, already. I have guests to entertain."

I got to my feet and started to follow him back. He slid his hand into mine, and I gave him a little squeeze. It was nice, and I was glad we'd come out into the woods. I would have been happier about it if we'd had sex out here too, but even though we didn't, I still enjoyed spending time with him.

"I'm a guest too," I reminded him as we neared the edge of the woods. There wasn't really a trail that we'd followed back, but the forest wasn't all that dense that close to the house either, so we didn't have any more trouble than the occasional large rock to step around or tree root to walk over.

"You're not a guest. You're a pain in my ass."

I licked my lips at his words as I remembered our night together. "Not recently," I teased. That got a smile from Caleb, but he also gave me the finger. I thought it was a pretty fair trade-off actually. As we neared his house, I saw Dean, Natalie, and Sam sitting together on Caleb's back deck.

"How long are they staying for?" I asked.

Caleb shrugged. I thought he'd let go of my hand once we were close enough to the house that they could see us, but he didn't let me go, and I wasn't willing to drop his hand until I absolutely had to either. "As long as they want. Sam is having a rough time at school since he told everyone he's gay."

"Brave kid."

"That's what I thought too."

I followed him back up to the front door instead of us saying good-bye at my car because I thought it would be good manners to say bye to them too. I shook Dean and Natalie's hands, gave Sam a wave, and was surprised with a whole pecan pie just for myself. "I can't.... It's too much," I told Natalie even as my mouth began to water over the idea of being able to eat it all on my own. And probably all in one afternoon too since no one would be there to stop me from indulging in what I was sure would become my next food obsession.

"Take the pie," Caleb told me as he put an arm around my shoulders.

Natalie nodded and surprised me by coming up and kissing me on my cheek. "You seem like a good boy for my Caleb."

"Woman, you keep calling him yours, and I'm going to start getting jealous," Dean announced.

I snickered, but I also had to shake my head to be able to correct her in her assumption. "We're not together."

She looked surprised for a minute before shaking her head at me. "You can play all you want, but I see how you look at him when you think he isn't looking."

I blushed and couldn't deny what she'd said, so I simply nodded and said, "Thanks for the pie." Then I turned to Caleb. "Saturday at six? I'll pick you up?"

Caleb gave me a smile. "Sure. I'll be ready. See you then."

I wanted to kiss him. I would have settled for a kiss on his cheek, or maybe even a hug, but I wasn't going to try that in front of them in case he rejected me. So I simply gave him a wave, said good-bye to everyone, and headed back home.

CHAPTER THIRTEEN

Caleb

BY 5:00 p.m. on Saturday, I was ready to go and anxiously sitting at my new dining room table—something I'd bought so we could have something to eat at—tapping my feet against the bottom rung of the chair I was sitting in. I still had an hour left to kill, but I was wearing my best jeans and a white button-down shirt with faint gray pinstripes and didn't want to go down to the barn just to get dirty. I'd hardly ever worn it and was really glad I still had it and that it fit, because I wanted to look nice for my first real date with Trent.

"Hey," Dean said as he came in the front door and sat down with me after grabbing a soda. He'd offered me one too, but I shook my head. I didn't want to spill it on me while I bounced around anxiously waiting for Trent to arrive. "Do you have a minute?"

I glanced up at the clock. I had fifty-three minutes left. "Yep. What's going on? Sam okay?"

Dean gave me a confused look. "Of course. Nat and I were talking, and I was hoping to see what you thought of something."

"Okay." I couldn't imagine why he seemed to be dancing around whatever he was trying to say to me. We'd been friends for years and years. He could have told me anything, and I wouldn't have minded.

"See, we're really happy here. We love the trees, the lack of traffic, being able to see the stars at night, not hearing a siren go off every few minutes when we're trying to sleep...."

I smiled because those were all the things I loved about Thornwood too. "Yeah. This place is pretty special."

"It is. And that's why we'd like to move here to Thornwood."

I stopped bouncing in my surprise. "That's fantastic!"

He still looked a bit worried, though, for some reason. "Thanks. We're pretty excited. Problem is, while we're looking for a new place to live, we were hoping to stay here with you for a little while longer. We'd also need some time to sell our place in LA and move our things out here."

A crazy, ridiculous idea came to me, but once I had it, I could hardly even begin to ignore it as I smiled at him. "Why not just stay here?"

"That's what I was asking you for...."

I shook my head. Apparently I hadn't made myself very clear at all. "No, I mean, why not just stay here? The huge garage would be easy to convert into a home for you all, and Nat could still homeschool Sam like she wants to, and I could teach him how to ride that fat horse out back." And my best friend would be living right nearby.

"That's a great offer, and I know Nat would love to, not to mention that Sam is in love with that horse, but we couldn't stay here. I'm sure you'd want to have your own space for...." He shrugged, but I knew what he was getting at. We both needed our private time. "And I wouldn't have us stay here rent free either."

I leaned forward and rested my elbows on the table. "How's this: Sam takes care of Magic and any other horses I decide to foster when Nat doesn't need him for other things, she can help cook sometimes, and you can help me mend fences and do upkeep. You know I have no idea what I'm doing when it comes to tools and stuff like that." I hoped he'd take me up on my offer. I wasn't asking him to work for me, and I would never have expected Natalie to sit there and make me each of my meals. I didn't need a chef, and I was perfectly capable of microwaving a frozen meal or baking a pizza, not that she'd let me eat any of my frozen pizzas since she'd come and taken over my kitchen, but I had hope that I'd be able to eat junk food again someday soon.

"I could convert the garage over to a house for you and save you all of the labor costs," he offered.

Honestly, I didn't give a damn about labor costs or anything else. I was just happy to have my friends, and the people I considered to really be my family more than my sister and her kids, possibly staying close to me. The only reason I might have stayed in LA was for Dean, but he'd been the one to tell me how much I needed to get out of the city and its toxic history for me.

"I'll talk it over with Nat. How soon do you want an answer?"

I shrugged. It didn't really matter to me. "Few years? Before Sam graduates from high school, maybe?"

He laughed and shook his head. "You're a good man, Caleb."

I didn't know if I necessarily agreed with him on that, but I was trying. I heard a car pull up to the house and looked up at the clock. Trent was five minutes early and I didn't even have to go check to make sure it was him. I knew the sound of his car by now, even when I heard him just driving down the main road. It was grittier, and louder, than a lot of the other cars in town. Most people in Thornwood seemed to have trucks that rumbled down the road like my old SUV. Trent had a nice car that was older but still powerful.

The doorbell rang, and I got up from the table. "How do I look?" I asked Dean.

He frowned and crossed his arms over his chest as he gave me a look. "You seriously asking?"

"Well... yes." I wouldn't have asked him if I wasn't actually wondering.

"You look fine. My wife would tell you that you worry too much. Damn, I hope you aren't still this nervous about dating when Sam starts. I don't want to have to reassure both of you."

I laughed, because Sam dating was a scary thought, and headed toward the front door. "Thanks, Dean. See you later. Talk to Nat."

He rolled his eyes at me. "Yeah, yeah. I'll talk to her." He shot me a grin as I opened the door to find Trent standing there with a six-pack of cinnamon rolls in his hands.

"Hi," I said, unsure about the cinnamon rolls but definitely interested if they tasted as good as they smelled.

Trent smiled at me. "Hey. I know flowers or chocolate are generally traditional. But these are from the diner and they taste better than any chocolate you can get in town."

I took them eagerly and went to the island to set them down.

"Hey, Dean," Trent said as he came in.

"You boys be good now. Have him back by nine," Dean joked.

I rolled my eyes before grabbing Trent's hand and pulling him out of the house. "You look great," I told Trent. He'd chosen jeans too, and the dark green sweater he had on looked really soft. After I grabbed his hand, and my fingers brushed against his cuff, I found out it was too.

"Thanks. So do you."

I expected him to say something else, like how I looked good enough to fuck or something along those lines, but he didn't. He just smiled at me as we got into his car, and once I'd buckled myself in, I took his hand again as he drove. "What'd you do today?" I asked.

"Cleaned, mostly. I couldn't really sit still." He shot me a grin, and I blushed, knowing that feeling really well. "You?"

"I invited Dean and his family to move in with me. Permanently."

I expected him to say something, to have an opinion about them living there. But what he did say surprised me. "Are you keeping Magic too, then?" He sounded so excited by that possibility that I just stared at him for a second.

"Why?"

He shrugged and shot me a quick smile before going back to paying attention to driving us down the main street of town. "I like seeing horses in those pastures again. And, remember, I told you I grew up going over to your barn and helping out with the horses?"

"I do remember that, and you probably know those woods better than me." I didn't mind that; in fact, it was sweet being able to picture a much younger Trent in my barn taking care of some horses there. If I'd lived in Thornwood when I was a teenager I probably would have been all over him. "And yeah, Magic's staying. Sam's in love with him."

Trent laughed and I smiled as I looked out the front window. He took me a little outside of Thornwood, to an Indian restaurant I'd been passing each time I went toward Denver but had never stopped in. "Is Indian okay?" he asked as he pulled into a parking space. "I probably should have asked you first."

It was cute that he blushed when he was uncertain about himself. I nodded and brushed my thumb over his knuckles. "Yeah, Indian food is good." I let go of his hand so we could get out of the car, but as soon as we were out, I grabbed him again. I was nervous, which wasn't unusual for me on a first date, but going out on a first date with Trent did feel a little strange. We'd kissed, we'd had sex, but at the same time I was just starting to get to know him too. We'd done things a bit backward, but that didn't really matter right then as we walked into the restaurant together.

"What made you change your mind about dating?" I asked after we'd ordered our drinks: hot chai for me and a mango lassi for him.

He gave me a little smile and reached across the table to take my hand again. We'd only separated to look over the drink menu. "I decided something."

"Oh?"

Trent nodded, and I waited for him to explain. But we were interrupted by the waiter bringing our drinks. We ordered our food, which was easy enough since I knew exactly what I wanted: chicken tikka masala. He ordered lamb curry, and we'd split some naan. By the time the waiter left, I was getting anxious wondering what he was going to be telling me.

"You were saying something?" I prompted him when he didn't start up again almost immediately after the waiter had walked away.

The restaurant was fairly busy, but tucked away in a booth in the corner like we were, it felt almost like it was just the two of us. I liked it a lot.

Trent caught my gaze from across the table. "Yeah. I was thinking that I like you, I want to be with you, and I'd like to get to know you better. I'm not over Simon. I'm going to need some time to deal with his death. I thought I would be able to be okay faster. For years I thought of him as being gone already. But I guess that at the back of my mind he was always there, even if he wasn't. And now that he's officially gone, it's hard for me to think of becoming that involved with someone again. I lost someone I loved, and I don't want to go through that again."

I understood where he was coming from and what he was saying. I'm sure it had been devastating for him to lose Simon. I couldn't even imagine it. I gave his hand a light squeeze and waited for him to continue without me pushing him along this time as he took a deep breath.

"You're the first person since Simon that I've wanted to spend time with. I'd love to have you naked all the time, but I don't absolutely need to be having sex with you to want to be near you. I want you as my friend, but I want you as more too. I thought Dean was your boyfriend when I first met him, and I was pretty jealous. I want you for myself, and it's not fair to ask you to wait around for me while I figure out how to have a relationship again."

I shook my head, because it wasn't and he was right. I also thought it was pretty funny that he thought I was with Dean. But I didn't say that.

Trent leaned down and kissed my knuckles. When he lifted his head again, I knew I was blushing pretty hard by how hot my cheeks were as I grinned at him. "I'm not saying I'll always get it right, or that we won't argue, but I'm going to try."

"I'm not asking you to be perfect," I said as I leaned toward him. "All I want is to know that I'm the only one you're with, that if we get to the point of saying 'I love you' to each other that I'm the only person you're saying it to. Don't cheat on me and don't lie to me. That's all I'm asking for."

He frowned and shook his head, and my gut tightened as I wondered if he was going to drop a bomb on me. Had he been with someone else recently? Last night? This morning even?

"You should be expecting a lot more than the bare minimum from someone," he said, surprising me out of my increasing worry and panic over the thought of him having sex with someone else on the day we were going to have our first date.

"I haven't had the best luck with guys," I told him honestly.

He laughed and shook his head. "I hate to tell you this, but your luck isn't improving all that much with me."

I shrugged. "I think I'd like to be the judge of that."

When our food came, we had to stop holding hands to be able to make scoops with the naan, but I didn't stop smiling at him, and when I offered him a bite of chicken off my fork, he took it instantly.

We skipped dessert and went back toward town for a movie. "Where's the theater?" I asked as I took his hand again. I hadn't seen a theater in town at all, but then again I hadn't driven around much outside of Thornwood either. I'd been too worried about getting lost in the mountains and eaten by the bears I was sure lurked somewhere in the woods just waiting to grab wayward city people like me.

"It's only a few miles up from the gas station where I saw you the first time," he said. And sure enough we passed the gas station and then pulled into an old theater. While the outside hadn't been maintained all that well, I noticed they were playing all the latest movies. Maybe it was the only theater around and all the little towns nearby used it. That's the only reason I could think of that a tiny town would have new movies to see.

"This isn't too far from town." I'd have to let Dean and Nat know about the theater since they liked movies as much as I did. They could go here for dates or Sam could go with some friends, after he made some in Thornwood of course.

161

Trent took my hand as we found our way toward the front door. He'd paid for dinner, and I hadn't minded, but now it was my turn to treat him. I pulled out some cash before he could even reach for his wallet and beat him to paying for the latest superhero movie. He grinned at me, I laughed, and soon enough we were sitting in a darkened theater with a box of candy between us and my hand resting loosely on his thigh.

"I want you," he whispered to me. The theater was mostly empty, with just a few people ten rows ahead of us and no one else around us where we sat in the very back of the theater where it was darkest. That had been his suggestion, not mine, but now I was wondering what he'd been planning.

"That's not a surprise," I whispered back to him with a smile.

He dragged my fingers along his inner thigh to where I felt the heavy weight of his cock pressing against the front of his jeans. I didn't pull my hand away, even though he was no longer hanging on to my wrist. But I didn't squeeze him either. Instead I barely touched him as I let my fingertips trace over the hard ridges I could feel just waiting for me if I wanted to unzip his pants. I was touching him so lightly I figured he might have thought it wasn't intentional. He put his arm around my shoulders and maybe he was trying to hold still, but he really wasn't doing a very good job of it at all as he squirmed under my hand.

"You're being a tease," he hissed at me.

"How? I'm not doing anything."

He groaned softly and leaned over to bite me on my neck. I nearly yelped, but luckily I was able to stop myself before I made the kind of noise that would definitely draw attention to us. "You know exactly what you're doing."

"Want me to stop, then?" I asked, already pulling my hand away. But he pushed it right back into place before I could go too far.

"No, I want you to do more."

I shook my head. "I don't put out on the first date." He laid his head on my shoulder and began gently sucking on my neck.

"I don't," I repeated, though his mouth on my skin was absolutely making me rethink my position on not having sex with him again right away. "Nope. Not happening."

He lifted his mouth off my neck, and I turned my head to kiss him. He shoved his tongue into my mouth and I moaned as softly as I could. "I want you under me," he breathed against my lips.

"I know. But right now we're in public and supposed to be watching a movie on our first date," I reminded him, though my resolve might as well have been a piece of paper that I'd torn up and thrown in the trash for all it mattered now. I wanted him too, first date or not. I wanted his hands on me, his mouth on my neck, his cock deep in me.

I gave him an involuntary squeeze just thinking about him being on top of me. And this time he couldn't hide his noises of pleasure so easily. "We should go," I said, already getting to my feet.

"But the movie. Our first date...."

I rolled my eyes, knowing he understood exactly what I was getting at. "We'll do a movie another time. Maybe when we're dragging ourselves out of bed after spending a weekend fucking each other senseless. Right now, though, a movie isn't happening."

"Damn straight." He looked pretty proud of himself as we hurried back to his car and he drove us to his townhouse. I was really glad he'd thought to go there instead of trying to get back to the house. Guests, especially with a kid around, and sex didn't really go together for me.

Not long after he closed the door behind me, I had my shirt off and tossed over the arm of his couch. His mouth was on mine a moment later, and we had collapsed onto the couch with him on top of me and pressing me into the soft cushions.

"Your 'no sex on the first date' rule didn't last long. Also, I don't like it," he said as he pulled off his shirt and lay back over me.

"It was more of a guideline than anything." I felt him sink his hips against mine, and I bit my lip as I clung to his shoulders. "You better have condoms."

He sucked on my neck and ran his hands down my sides in a frenzied pattern, like he couldn't get enough of touching me, like he needed to feel every inch of me. I hoped that was what he was feeling since that was exactly how I felt as I dug my fingers into the thick muscles of his shoulders.

"I do, and lube too. Fuck, Caleb, I need you," he groaned against my neck.

"Me too." Pretending otherwise would have never worked. The best thing for both of us was just to accept how this was going to be between us. "I still want to go out on dates," I told him as I reached for the button of his jeans. "We won't always have sex." I didn't want him to have that idea in his head.

"Sure. Not always, only 90 percent of the time."

He helped me undo his pants, then got to work on mine. "That's reasonable," I agreed. He was beautiful with clothes on, but I loved seeing him naked with his abs on full display for me. Before he could get back on top of me, I leaned forward and ran my tongue over the muscles of his stomach. His cock bobbed against my chin, and he pushed his hand into my hair. Knowing exactly what he wanted, I looked up at him as I kissed down his stomach.

He groaned and smiled a little at me as I swirled my tongue around the tip of his already wet cock. I rested my hands on his hips. Closing my eyes, I opened my lips a little to take his head in and was treated to his groan of pleasure. I also got a hiss as I brushed my teeth lightly along the underside of his head, making him jerk against my mouth.

He pushed me down, gently at first as if he was testing me, seeing how I'd react to him having control of my head. I was pretty sure I surprised him by taking him all the way down to his base and humming against him, though, because he jumped and I felt him spray a little into the back of my throat. I swallowed him and let him take over, welcoming his control over me until he pulled me off and I ran the back of my hand across my mouth.

I knew I was good, and I'd been complimented before, but it was nothing like seeing the heat in his eyes or the way he didn't speak, like he couldn't get the words out, as he turned me over on the couch and knelt behind me. He got a condom, and I listened as he put it on before something cold was squirted on my hole. I yelped and glared over my shoulder at him. "Give me some warning next time. Damn, that's cold."

He gave me a grin before he leaned forward and kissed me at the base of my spine. "Sorry. I am putting lube into your asshole now so that I may fuck you as hard as I want. Next I will begin stretching you. And then I will—"

"Jerk," I shot back at him as I smiled.

He laughed, and I rested my head on my arms as he stuck his fingers slowly inside of me. More lube was added until he apparently felt I was ready for him. By then I was so impatient that I just wanted him in me. If I wasn't completely stretched it would be a little uncomfortable, at first, but not having him inside of me was torture in itself, and I wasn't sure which would have been worse. Trent came up against me, and I smiled into my arms as I felt him push inside me. We both moaned, and I hung on to the edge of the cushion as he grabbed my hips and went deeper. He still wasn't all the way in, like I wanted him to be, but he was getting there and it didn't take him long to get the rest of the way.

He found a pace that worked for him, and I moaned each time he thrust into me and pulled my hips back to meet him. He grabbed my hair, yanking me back. He ran his hands down my spine, and I was sure he'd left scratch marks, because I felt hot streaks going down my skin. I couldn't wait to look at myself in the mirror when we were done. I reached between my legs and began stroking myself when my own pleasure built too high for me to try to hang on any longer. Trent wrapped an arm around my shoulder as I shot onto the floor. We kissed, awkward as it was, and he nipped at my jaw as I panted.

"Tell me to go harder," he gasped out.

"Fuck me harder," I said quickly. My orgasm had been a surprise, not just the speed of it but also the strength. If he hadn't been in me, holding me up, I wasn't sure I'd still be able to kneel.

He kissed me again, then bit down on my shoulder as he pounded into me. "I love it when you beg. Always do that."

Sweaty, sated, and completely happy, I smiled back at him. "You can bite me wherever, whenever you want." That was a huge turn-on for me.

He nodded, and then there was nothing more for him to say as he groaned and jerked inside of me as he came. We separated a few minutes later, but neither of us moved from the floor when we collapsed in his living room. I was a sweaty mess, but I didn't really care as I lay there grinning like a lunatic up at the ceiling.

"Dates with you are the best," he said as he pulled me close and laid his hand on my chest. He was still breathing heavily, as was I, and it was good to know I affected him just as much as he did me.

I laughed and shook my head. "We'll need to actually get through a date sometime here soon before you decide that." I reached up to take his hand.

"Stay over tonight, and I'll take you out to breakfast and the zoo tomorrow. That'll be like a date," he offered. It was easy to agree to that date with him, and luckily we actually managed to make it all the way through it that time.

Sometimes it wasn't easy with Trent. There were plenty of times where I did want to strangle him for being stupid. But he never lied to me, and never cheated on me. And when he told me he loved me I knew I was the only one he was saying it to.

Keep reading for an exclusive excerpt from

About Last Night

By Caitlin Ricci

A Thornwood Novel

Before jumping into his first semester of college, Thomas Maloney decides to lose his virginity at a party to a stranger he's sure he'll never see again. Only the next day, he's surprised to learn the same one night stand will be sharing his dorm room. Thomas considers himself lucky, but his new roommate—not so much.

Closeted as they come, football jock Remington "Rem" Daniels fears if he requests a room change his dad will grow suspicious. On track for a shot at the pros, Rem tries to play it cool and avoid falling for the confidently gay Thomas. Dealing with their constant need to get in bed together wouldn't be so hard if Rem didn't have a girlfriend and Thomas didn't have a conscience.

When she delivers news that will change Rem's life forever, Thomas knows it's time to move back home to Thornwood, Colorado. But neither the distance nor knowing Rem belongs to someone else helps Thomas get over him. Rem's feelings haven't changed either. When it comes down to love or football, Rem will have to make the hardest choice of his life and hope Thomas will still be waiting for him when he does.

Chapter One

LOSING MY virginity to a stranger the night before my first semester in college was probably the stupidest idea my friends and I had ever come up with. And I wished they were here with me now as I fixed a simple black mask over my face and headed up the steps to what was supposed to be the best party on campus for the whole year. My friends, stuck in Colorado while I was here in Miami, would have egged me on, they would have been encouraging. I could have stood by them and laughed like I actually had some friends instead of coming into the fraternity and standing awkwardly in the corner with a drink someone had pushed into my hand.

Just because I was from a small town in the Colorado mountains didn't mean that I'd never had a drink before, but I wasn't big on them. If I really was going to go through with this though, I knew I'd need some courage, so I started drinking whatever it was in big gulps. It hurt and it burned but I was able to keep it down and when I was done with my first I grabbed another. Smiling at the people around me was easier after that first drink. Laughing came next and talking about classes, the Miami humidity, and how I'd only just seen the ocean for the first time was almost fun.

I'd never been all that great at dancing, but with the alcohol working its way through me, that didn't seem to matter so much anymore. Rock mixed with punk which bled quickly into pop as the house thumped around me. People laughed and I danced with anyone who wanted to be close to me. Maybe if I'd been sober, or had less outgoing friends, maybe then the idea of getting rid of my virginity before anyone found out that I hadn't had sex yet wouldn't have made as much sense. But the guys had told me about how all their college friends only wanted them because they thought they were cute and inexperienced, and how I didn't want to lose my virginity to someone like that.

As the night wore on it started to make more and more sense to me. I was eighteen, fairly cute according to my friends, and if I wasn't worried about who to give my virginity to, and making it count as something important, then I could have fun and not be worried about dating, or who I was having sex with now that I wasn't living at home.

I saw the perfect guy sitting on the kitchen island. His legs dangled over the side and he had a drink in his hand too. My third, maybe, was nearly out and I'd come in to see about getting another. This guy had nice, thick thighs, a bit of hair showing under his shorts, and a Miami COllege tshirt on. It was purple, just like the mask he had on that hid most of his face from me. It did nothing to cover up the bright bleach blond hair sticking up all over his head, or his pretty green eyes.

I danced up to him, thinking I looked cool as hell and he just laughed at me. We were alone in the kitchen, for the moment, when I moved between his legs and leaned up to kiss him. My glass fell over the side of the counter and he had to have put his down somewhere because he put his arms around me and then his tongue went into my mouth. I sucked on his lower lip and rubbed my stomach against the front of his shorts. He never pushed me away, never even seemed like he might not have been interested, and I thought he was practically perfect.

We traded kisses with my hands on the tops of his thighs until people came into the kitchen. We broke apart then, and I was feeling a little dizzy, but when he took my hand and pulled me through the house, past couples making out over every inch of available space, and into a large closet, I didn't worry about a thing.

We kept kissing and he ran his hands over me as roughly as he could, as if he couldn't get enough of me. That's the same way I felt about him in that moment, like I needed everything and then some, like there wasn't enough air in the closet and I was burning up. He reached for my pants but I had my hands on his first and dropped to my knees in front of him. Without a word I took him into my mouth, sliding my lips over his thick head, as he rested his hands on the back of my head. He didn't push me down, didn't try to control me in any way, just rested there as I licked up the underside of his cock and jacked him with one hand while touching myself with the other.

After a few minutes, and getting to taste his salty pre-cum, I got up and he turned me around, pushing me onto something hard, and I realized it wasn't a closet we were in, but actually the laundry room. Huh. I'd never considered my first time to be while I was bent over a dryer. But it didn't really bother me either. I was grinning as he pushed down my pants and spread me open for him.

At least one of us was sober enough to remember to use a condom, I thought as I heard him tear one open. A little stretching, not nearly as much as I needed but at least the alcohol dulled the pain, and then I felt him inside of me. I gasped, he groaned, and I leaned forward as he put one hand on my shoulder, right next to my neck, and the other on my hip.

I was lucky to find someone that was gay, bi, or too drunk to care right off the bat. And god he was hot too, all hard muscle and strong fingers that gripped my shoulder.

"Oh fuck," he groaned, the first words he'd said to me.

I laughed, though it came out as more of a pant, and nodded as he fucked me against the dryer. I'd be sore in the morning, I was sure, but right then, in that moment, I thought everything was wonderful. My friends were right, this was the best way to lose my virginity. And, even with my limited experience in the department, I thought purple mask guy was fucking amazing.

"Right there," I gasped out when he hit something inside of me that felt pretty perfect.

He hit it again and I shook. He laughed and I leaned all the way onto the dryer and gripped it as tight as I could, my fingers curling around the edges and becoming nearly as white as the metal.

It didn't matter that I didn't know his name, or what he looked like, or anything else about him. It was almost better, actually. There were no expectations here, no complications either. It was just pleasure and excitement.

The cold metal bled into me, mixing with the heat of my skin, and I instantly loved the mixed feeling it created along my skin. He moved his hand from my shoulder to the back of my hair as he got closer. I was pretty sure, from the times I'd jacked off with my friends, that his jerky, erratic movements probably meant that he was getting close, and I grabbed my cock to keep up with him. I wanted to come too, and with him in me still. I sped up, nearly to the point where I'd be causing myself pain, before I released with a shudder onto the front of the dryer.

I was still a bit limp as I recovered when he pushed himself all the way inside of me and yanked back on my hair. He pumped into me and I could feel his cock pulsing inside of me as he held me there. After a few seconds he let my hair go and I slumped forward.

I thought he'd leave me for sure after that. We were done, but he apparently wasn't, as he turned me back over and helped me sit up on the dryer. It was cold on my ass, but he warmed me right up again with his rough kisses.

"Thanks," I said to him, when he let me up to breathe.

"Yeah. You too."

He gave me another kiss, and licked at my bottom lip, before leaving me in that laundry room. I didn't go after him, didn't try to find him again at the party, just cleaned up my mess with a rag I tossed into the washer as soon as I was done, fixed my pants, then walked back to my hotel.

I was moving into the dorms in the morning and felt pretty good about the night I'd had. It was nearly eleven, but in Colorado it was only getting to nine, so once I was back in my hotel room, and showered, I called my mom.

"Hey, sweetie pie. How's Miami?" she asked me as soon as she picked up.

I tossed the towel I'd been using on my hair to the side and stretched out on the bed. "Pretty decent. Lots of humidity. And a lot of people in this hotel seem to have little dogs. Maybe it's a Miami thing because I'm pretty sure no one in town has a dog under five pounds back home."

My mom laughed and it was good to hear her voice. "No. I think we'd call them bear food if someone did. Oh, your cousin Trent says hello."

He wasn't really my cousin. My mom just worked at the same diner, and had been working there for the past twenty years, that Trent's mom had owned. We were cousins because our moms had been best friends before his mom had passed. "Say hi back for me, please."

I liked Trent. He was a cop but he didn't pull us over unless we were being stupid. I hadn't had a car when I'd left town for Miami so my record was thankfully clean. But a lot of my friends had had to take summer jobs to pay off their tickets for being reckless.

I hoped that she couldn't tell I'd been drinking, or that I was probably pretty drunk. I'd only been really drunk a few times before but I was pretty sure this was one of them. I didn't feel sick, yet, but I knew I needed to take some pain killers tonight to hold off what was certainly coming for me in the morning. Whatever, it would be completely worth it for the night I'd had.

"Are you staying out of trouble?"

I laughed. "Yeah. More or less."

She laughed with me and I was glad we had the kind of relationship that, if I'd wanted to, I could have told her about my night and she would have only worried about me using protection. She was really cool like that. "Your dad made you a mixed tape, CD, mp3 thing… anyway. It's all the songs about Miami that he could find. He's going to send it to you in the mail. Some of them though…. Thomas, honey, there are days I'm glad you are only interested in boys."

I shook my head as I laughed. "Men mom. I'm eighteen. I like men now. Not boys." I put my forehead over my eyes and stared up at the ceiling.

"Oh excuse me. Look who's all grown up now just because they got to move out. Well, I'm glad you like men then, because some of these songs about women and their thongs and booties. I may not be on top of all of what you kids do or know but even I know that when that song said booty it wasn't talking about those cute little socks I knitted for Elijah."

"Yeah. Probably not. How's the baby anyway?" He was almost a year now, my little foster brother. I called him a baby, because he was so tiny, but really he was getting up there and growing a bit more everyday.

I heard the sadness in my mom's voice and could picture her frown as if I was sitting right there next to her. "Oh, you know. He's a handful. Those damn drugs...."

I nodded. I'd taken my first sip of alcohol with my friends in one of their dad's man caves while we were in middle school, but I'd been really careful never to get involved with any kinds of drugs because I saw what they did to the babies my mom fostered. It wasn't that I planned to ever have kids, biologically anyway, but I just didn't want to be a part of something that hurt babies so much.

"Yeah. I know. I'm sure it's tough. Are you still thinking about taking in those brothers too?" I asked her. My mom was always fostering more kids. There were a few that she'd adopted over the years, like me, but most of them were only with her during their court cases or before they got placed with a family member.

"Oh you know, with you out of the house, it seems like someone should be using your room. I can't very well make Saturday morning pancake shapes for just your dad and I."

God I missed Saturday morning pancakes already. My mom put cinnamon in the pancakes then dusted them with sugar. She used real butter too, the kind she made from shaking heavy whipping cream in a mason jar until it got all hard. My stomach growled, even though I'd had a cheeseburger, and I rubbed it. I'd only been gone a few days but I was already missing home.

"I can't wait to come have them again. Missing you and dad already." I frowned, wondering if I'd really been ready to move across the country. I'd considered any of the colleges in Denver, but I'd wanted to be by the ocean and see something more than the mountains for once.

"Oh honey, we miss you too. Don't you worry, I'll still be making pancakes when you come back for fall break. Or winter break, or whenever really. Don't feel like you need to rush back home. Go, have an adventure. Fall in love, break some hearts, taste the ocean for me."

I wiped at my eyes, because they were blurry, and realized I was crying without even meaning to or realizing I was doing it. "Love you, Mama."

"Love you too, Thomas. Now, it's after eleven there, if this world clock we set to Miami time is correct, so I'm going to let you go get some rest so that you can move in bright and early tomorrow. Take pictures for me and make sure to lift with your legs, not your back. You don't need to be rushed to the emergency room before school even starts. Blow up something in the chemistry lab first."

I grinned and sighed. "You'd be so worried."

"But I would also have the first son in Thornwood to blow up a chemistry lab. Think of that now. All the ladies at the diner asked about you today. They think you'll come back all tanned and ready for their daughters. Come back with some handsome man instead. That'll show them."

"I'll try," I promised her. Still smiling, I thought about the guy from the party. Of course I'd never see him again, but it had been fun. If she told her diner friends about what I'd done that would certainly give them something to talk about, or more like gossip about, in the tiny town I'd lived in all my life before coming here. "Talk to you later." I yawned, really feeling the time now.

"Night, baby. You take care of yourself and remember to send me pictures."

"I will. I will. Promise." We blew each other kisses through the phone and I hung up. A couple of pain pills later, and an old movie on the TV to help me go to sleep, and I was out less than an hour later.

CAITLIN RICCI was fortunate growing up to be surrounded by family and teachers who encouraged her love of reading. She has always been a voracious reader and that love of the written word easily morphed into a passion for writing. If she isn't writing, she can usually be found studying as she works toward her counseling degree. She comes from a military family, and the men and women of the armed forces are close to her heart. She also enjoys gardening, hiking, and horseback riding in the Colorado Rockies where she calls home with her wonderful fiancé and their two dogs. Her belief that there is no one true path to happily ever after runs deeply through all of her stories.

Website: www.CaitlinRicci.com

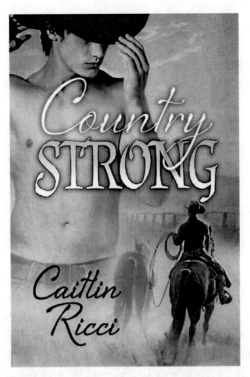

With only three months left on a lease-to-own agreement on a quarter horse Wyatt's worked hard to own, a thunderstorm spooks General and he throws Wyatt, changing both their lives forever. Luckily, Kellen, a friend of the stable owner, calls for emergency medical attention, and Wyatt comes out of the hospital with a broken wrist and a concussion.

When Wyatt returns to the stable, he finds the owner has sold General to Kellen for retraining. But Wyatt's woes have just begun, and now he must drive an hour to see his horse. The perks help balance the hardships, however, and Wyatt finds himself falling for Kellen. His fortitude is soon tested again by the ultimate betrayal when he learns Kellen doesn't intend to return General after he's trained.

www.dreamspinnerpress.com

Charlie thinks his Friday will be the same as any other working as an animator, until Quinn Fitzgerald and his rescued Asiatic Lion, Aseem, walk into the studio. While the lion is impressive, his handler is the real reason Charlie's heart skips a beat.

Quinn has devoted years of his life to rescuing big cats, so he can't turn down the donation the animation company is offering in exchange for using one of his cats as a model.

Charlie isn't quite as confident as the handsome, charming man his sister teasingly calls Sex God Quinn Fitzgerald. He's so nervous he can hardly talk to the other man, so he's shocked when Quinn not only notices him but invites him to spend the weekend at his big cat sanctuary.

www.dreamspinnerpress.com

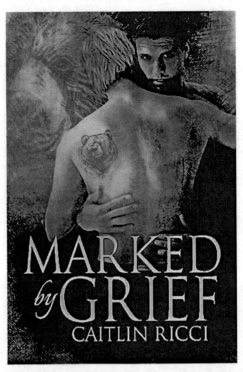

Six months after Kit lost his big brother to a drunk driver, he's alone and feeling like everyone has left him behind. He struggles to get out of bed, to feed himself, to talk to his parents. Worst of all, the man he loves, his brother's best friend, hasn't spoken to him since the funeral.

Tattoo artist Jason always planned to wait until Kit was a bit more experienced and mature before he told Kit how he felt about him. But Bear's death changes everything, and Jason opts to give Kit space to heal.

However, the next time they meet, Jason is startled at how far Kit has deteriorated, so he takes him home. Simply taking care of Kit isn't enough. Marking Kit with the tattoo he demands opens a window, but Jason still isn't getting through, until he begins ordering Kit around and sees how receptive Kit is to his strong hand.

www.dreamspinnerpress.com

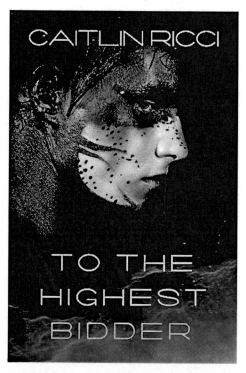

The Intergalactic Star Pilot Academy has accepted Thierry Leroux into the elite class of sky year 2231. But the academy comes with a hefty price tag, and there's no way he, a poor Sythe orphan, has the credits the academy requires. Thierry's brother, Corbin, a high-class companion, suggests Thierry sell his virginity for the cost of tuition. It seems like a ridiculous idea, but it may be Thierry's only shot, so Thierry asks Corbin to arrange a meeting on the pleasure planet of Wish.

On Wish, Thierry meets Corbin's boss, Monroe, and they agree to auction off Thierry's virginity. Thierry is grateful to the masked buyer he knows only as "Dragonfly," and Dragonfly is gentle, making Thierry's first time a good memory. When Dragonfly requests to see him again, and pay for the pleasure, Thierry returns to Wish. But in this game, falling in love is dangerous for the heart, and Thierry might not like the man behind the mask.

www.dreamspinnerpress.com

A Forever Home: Book One

Werewolves are real. Marius enjoys the irony that everyone calls him a dog whisperer, not just because he's a werewolf, but for his work at the local animal shelter. He has a unique talent for pairing families with their perfect pets upon first meeting them. But he's still looking for acceptance and a forever family of his own. Then Jack comes into the rescue looking for a big, mean dog. To prevent Jack from making the wrong choice, Marius convinces him to adopt a needy spaniel mix instead. But when Marius learns Jack is tormented by horrible memories while at his apartment, he opens his home to the sweet, scared man. As their relationship grows, Jack feels comfortable telling Marius about the horrors he suffered. Marius hopes his steady presence, protection, and love can help Jack reclaim the pieces of himself broken on that terrible night.

www.dreamspinnerpress.com

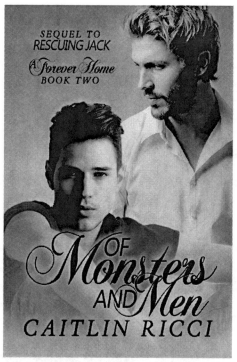

A Forever Home: Book Two

Seth's life looks idyllic on the surface. He has a great job at the pet rescue with a fantastic boss, who happens to be a werewolf. He is getting his degree at the local university and has a best friend who understands that the most intimate thing for Seth is a kiss. But when it comes to relationships, Seth's perfect life is a jumbled mess. No guy stays around because eventually, they always want more than Seth, who is asexual, is able to give. Seth wants love and a relationship, but not the sex that everyone puts so much value on.

Seth tries for something more with the man he has a crush on, but when that ends Seth feels like he's back to square one. So when his boss's brother, Jeremy, pushes his way into Seth's life, insisting that he won't press for more than Seth is comfortable sharing, Seth is wary. All of Seth's experience says it won't last long. But Jeremy is one werewolf who is used to getting his way, and might just be patient enough to wait for Seth to see he means what he says.

www.dreamspinnerpress.com

ONE MARINE,
Hero

EM LYNLEY

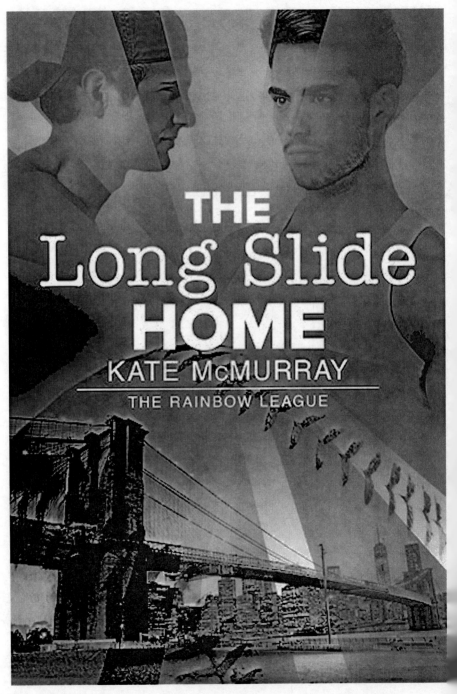

THE
Long Slide
HOME
KATE McMURRAY
THE RAINBOW LEAGUE

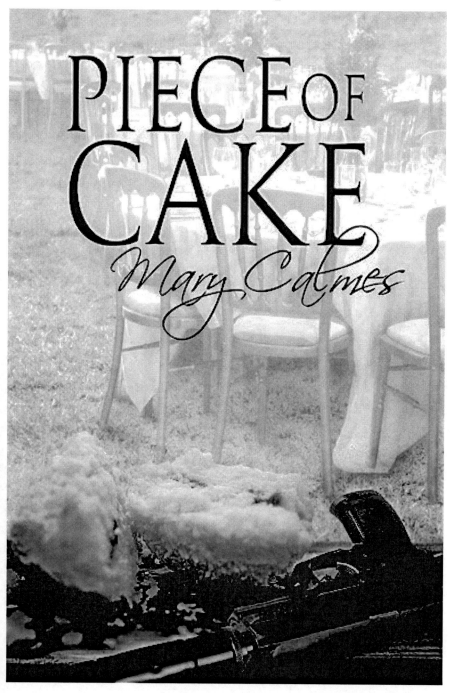

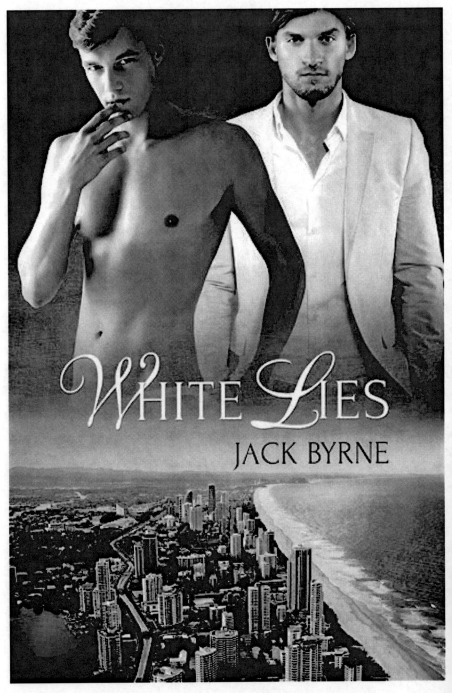

Also from Dreamspinner Press

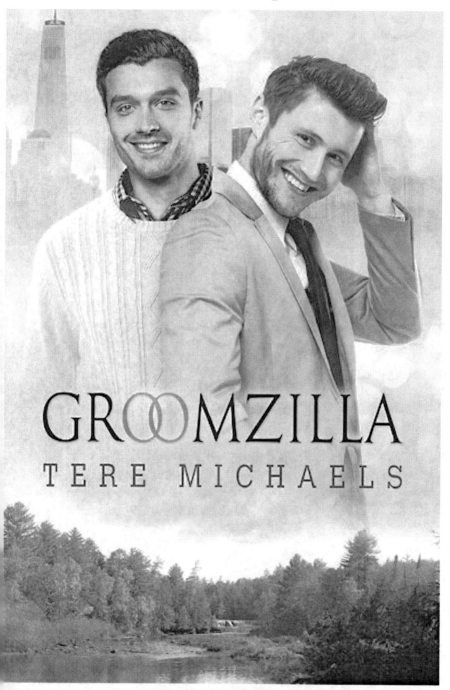

GR∞MZILLA
TERE MICHAELS

www.dreamspinnerpress.com